The film version of **Virgin Witch** is available on video from Redemption Films.

For a full list of all Redemption Books and videos please send a standard sized SAE to:-
The Redemption Centre,
PO Box 50,
Stroud, Gloucs.,
England GL6 8YG.

Virgin Witch
by Klaus Vogel

REDEMPTION
BOOKS

First published in the UK
by Corgi Books, 1971.
This edition published by Redemption Books, 1995.
A divsion of Redemption Films Limited,
BCM PO Box 9235, London WC1N 3XX.

A catalogue record for this book is available
from the British Library.

ISBN 1 899634 20 7

Printed in the UK by
The Guernsey Press Company Limited.
Cover and photographic section printed by
Colin Clapp Printers.

The logs spit out sparks. The flames crackle. The dry grass burns. The fire is night's only light, exciting the leaves into blood-reds and golds as if autumn has come artificially early. It turns the trees into scenery; unreal, like dark cut-outs with nothing behind them. The clearing is a stage where a strange performance is being enacted.

Cowled figures gather so tightly that they obscure the focal point of their intent. A girl's stifled gasps punctuated by an unheeded cry for help are the only indication.

The figures stand erect. Slowly they begin to back away into a circle, their preparations nearly complete. A young girl is stretched out on the ground, as if on a crucifix, her wrists bound by leather thongs attached to stakes driven into the earth. Fear of the unknown haunts her eyes, but she no longer struggles, resigned that it is to no avail.

The leader intones an incomprehensible chant and the others take it up in the summer night's air. The circle begins to sway, the chant becomes more intense. At a sign from the leader, two of his followers kneel and hold the girl's ankles. Then, as the leader takes a pace towards her feet, they force them apart and tie them off to two more stakes. Now she lies spread-eagled, helpless as sacrificial lamb.

The leader's ceremonial dagger flashes in the firelight. The incantation pulsates faster and faster as he steps forward until his bare feet touch the insides of her calves. Her eyes are hypnotised by the blade's sharp point. She tries to scream but no sound will come. She gulps in air to try again. From high above the leader's head, the dagger begins a slow ritual plunge towards her naked body. It makes a long arc between the hills of her breasts. Her violent breathing almost causing it to end its journey there. Then the leader pulls it down across her navel, and plunges it finally into the earth between her legs.

The incantation stops. The assembled figures throw off their robes and link hands - male, female, male, female. Then they point incisively at the dagger's jewelled hilt. They link again, circling anti-clockwise.

The leader kneels down, withdraws the blade and throws it away. Two men break the circle momentarily to step forward and remove his robe. Then, as the incantation rises to a crescendo, the leader stretches his length upon the girl. She closes her eyes as the full realisation of what the initiation will mean comes home to her.

Now her scream is released and it rends the air, absorbed by the tress before it reaches outside ears. Again and again she cries out. The screams turn to groans, grow quieter, softer, and soon to barely-heard moans of pleasure. It is as she was told it would happen. She has run the gamut from fear to ecstasy. Another witch has been initiated.

I t was one of those rare nights when the full moon shines unobscured from a midnight blue sky. No clouds hid the stars or interrupted the moon's cold glow. Christine had never seen it quite like that before - at least she had never felt it's power so strongly. She felt compelled to stare at its blemished face; as if it were a boy whose attraction she couldn't resist in spite of his acne. In contrast, the moonlight made her own pure skin seem translucent and her eyes shone with an inner light of their own.

Her sister stood only a few yards away on the grass verge of the busy road. But Betty was far from being lost in the same enchantment. She was getting more and more anxious as she thumbed unsuccessfully at vehicles that screeched past so close that she sometimes had to take a step back for safety. A clutch of lorries clattered by, nose to tail, their throbbing engines almost deafening her. But Christine did not seem to hear them.

Every now and then there was a lull, usually followed by a solitary car hurtling towards them from the North, its headlights barely having time to pick them up before it began to disappear again into the night. They all seemed hell-bent to get somewhere fast before dawn. Only the Lane sisters were not making any progress.

'Oh come on, Chris,' Betty complained. 'You help too. Don't just leave it to me.'

Betty knew nothing of the art of hitching lifts. That the trick was to take up a position where the road forced cars to slow down. That most drivers would stop gladly for two dolly birds if it was on. Christine's white coat profiled her figure and revealed her lovely legs that sent sex-impulses through many windscreens. And a momentary flash of Betty's waif-like smile pleading 'Please give us a lift' stirred lecherous thoughts in lusty-minded drivers eager to take advantage. But by the time the facts had registered the opportunity had gone. The girls were receding fast, other blokes' headlights lighting on them. Only a madman would dare stop and back up, running the risk of being smashed from behind. Some drivers slowed and then sped up again. There'd be other birds. There always were.

Lorry drivers had schedules and there were plenty of scrubbers to be found at the pull-in places. Others, more self-right-

CHAPTER ONE

eous, knew that girls weren't up to any good at that time of night. One or two knew for certain they must be 'on the game'. But they were wrong.

Betty was tiring; thumbing automatically and looking anxiously at Christine. She had seen this expression on her sister's face before. The light from the moon, intermingled with harsh headlights, made her look very strange indeed. Betty hesitated to disturb her. Chris was miles away - gone into one of her trances as Dad would have said. In her white coat, her face upturned and serene, she looked like a novitiate about to take her vows. That was how she looked...

Then, as if Betty had only just that second called her, Christine came down to earth: 'You're not thumbing every single one, are you? We don't want a lorry. That's a terrible way to get there. Pick a nice big car. You know, luxury.'

'Pick? I'd be thankful for anything! While you've been dreaming hundreds have gone past and nobody wants to know. I don't want to stand here all night. We should have started in the morning - like I said.'

Christine was dogmatic. 'I told you at home. We go tonight. I wasn't putting up with him a minute longer. Nor you.'

Betty sighed. 'Why do I always have to do what you say?'

Christine smiled, the way she knew never failed to win Betty over. 'Because I'm older than you are. Ten whole minutes older!' Then she went serious and sincere. 'Stick with me, Betty. I'll make it go right. You'll see.' And Betty knew she meant it.

It always infuriated Christine when anyone said to them: 'You don't look a bit like twins, really.' As if they should. They were close, but different. And Betty would always be guided by her. She always had been, even when they were little. Now they were on their own, she might have to be even more dominant.

'Well, let's see what you can do, then. Go on! Pick up a luxury car,' challenged Betty. 'No one's going to stop for me. Not unless I pull up my skirt and show my legs. And I don't intend to do that.' Once again she raised her thumb as a lone lorry past without even slowing down.

As if on impulse Christine pulled Betty's arm down. 'I told

you - we're not going in one of those smelly things.'

'Chris, don't be fussy! Beggars can't be choosers.'

Suddenly Christine stopped and pointed North where the dark was stabbed by two pairs of headlights approaching fast. 'We're not beggars. Don't ever think we are. We'll take this one!'

To Betty's amazement, Chris walked out into the road and held up her hand in the recognised 'stop' sign. It was suicide.

'Chris! Come back! You'll be killed!'

'No, I won't.' Christine calmly pushed the palm of her hand against the fierce beams as if expecting to stop them dead.

The last thing Johnny Dixon was expecting to see in his Jaguar's long-throw lights was a gorgeous young thing with smashing legs and a tight white coat slap bang in the middle of the road coming up at a rate of knots. What was she, some sort of nut? He'd been driving for over an hour and was used to night traffic. Far less stuff about than by day, and you got early warning from other blokes' lights. Everybody else in kip so you could forget about pedestrians.

He'd been fully relaxed, slumped back in the leather squab, one hand on the wheel, his shoe resting lightly on the accelerator pedal to keep the machinery gunning at a steady seventy-eight plus on the straight stretches, like this one. Now he alerted, grabbed the wheel, gauged the distance and pressed on the brake pedal, gradually increasing the friction as the radials bit into the tarmac and held. But it was on the edge all the way down the speedo; fifty-forty-thirty-twenty-ten. He blew a toneless whistle in relief when he saw he was going to make it. 'Thank God for discs all around.'

Like its animal namesake, the Jaguar lurched as it stopped dead. Then Johnny swung the wheel and eased it onto the verge for safety as Christine walked to the side, her long dark hair shot through by moonlight. Betty held back warily as Johnny leaned across and wound down the window. He couldn't believe his eyes. Not only one dolly, but two. And no boyfriends coming into sight! He'd seen that dodge before and was ready to move off fast if they did.

'Something wrong?' Johnny played it fatherly for a start. He was nearing thirty and these two were just a couple of kids.

'Going to London?' Christine, of course.

'That your idea of hitching? Blimey, I thought someone'd been murdered.' Johnny never wrapped up his Cockney, even on first acquaintance. If you didn't like it, you could do the other.

'We weren't getting anywhere just thumbing.' Christine smiled and the dark brooding expression lightened up attractively.

'That was a mad thing to do! Good job I'm a bit of a Jackie Stewart. You're too young to die.'

Christine ignored the banter. 'Can you help?'

'Sure. Hop in!'

Betty pointed behind them. 'Just a minute. I'll get our cases.'

Christine left her to it, sliding into the back seat of the Jaguar as if she did it every day. In a flash of lorry headlights Johnny saw Betty lugging two large suitcases and jumped out to help her.

'I'll take 'em darlin', you'll do yourself a mischief. Cor! What's in 'em? All your worldly goods?'

'Just about! Thanks. I'm stronger than I look, though. You'd be surprised.'

'Would I now?' Johnny stacked the cases on the back seat next to Christine, who was reclining in the luxury upholstery. Johnny couldn't help jibing: 'Won't be in your way at all, will they miss? Or should I put them in the boot?'

Christine took him literally. 'No, they're not worrying me. Hurry up, Betty. Get in.'

Johnny couldn't help grinning as he opened the front passenger door, inviting Betty to ride next to him. She smiled her thanks. No one had ever held a car door for her before and she didn't take it for granted.

As he moved the Jag up through the gears, Johnny asked: 'Running away from home, then?' The fast acceleration up to seventy seemed to accentuate the question.

Betty tried to hedge. 'Well...not really...' But Christine felt there was nothing to hide. 'Yes, that's exactly what we're doing.'

Until then Betty had only noticed how good-looking Johnny was. Now she took in his clothes - a bit flashy with the jewelled tie-clip, the turned-back jacket-cuffs, the buckled shoes. 'How did you guess?' she queried.

'Classic, innit? Middle of the night. Suitcases. Wanna go to London. You're not lorry girls, even I can see that. Stands out a mile. You're running away, right.'

'No law against it, is there?' Betty tried to justify their action.

'Nothing to do with me if there is. How old are you?'

Christine, looking out of the window, must have been listening after all. 'Seventeen.'

'Only just, I'll bet.' Johnny glanced at Betty. She did look very young.

'Both of us! We're twins,' she confirmed.

'And don't say you can't tell or I'll scream,' added Christine. 'We're not identical - we're different as chalk and cheese.' Christine meant in appearance but already Johnny could tell it went deeper than that.

Johnny's voice took on a scolding edge. 'Know it all, don't you. Kids! Didn't your parents ever tell you anything? Don't you read the Sunday papers?'

Betty was slow to follow his logic-jump. 'Read what in the papers?'

'Come off it. You can't be that innocent! What happens to girls who get picked up in cars? In daylight - never mind this hour of the morning. You're asking for it and you know it.'

Betty defended their characters. 'We're not asking for anything except a lift. We can look after ourselves. There's two of us. You don't think I'd do this on my own? Or Chris - would you?' She turned to her sister in the back of the car.

Christine was still looking through the window, the moon striking obliquely across her face. She seemed oblivious of her front-seat companions.

Johnny laughed briefly. 'There's plenty of girls younger than you walking the streets - just 'cos they believed there was safety in numbers. You didn't know I was on my tod when you did your suicide act, did you? Could have been two fellers, three, four, in this wagon. Then what?'

Christine did not alter her gaze. 'I knew you'd be on your own. And that you're not the nasty kind...'

Betty added: 'And we wouldn't have got in, neither.'

'How d'you know I'm not a raving sex-maniac? They don't jump on you the minute they clap eyes on you. They concentrate on their driving, innocent like, looking for a nice lonely spot where you won't be heard if you turn out to be a screamer. Just watch yourselves, that's all I'm saying. You never know. Particularly these days.'

He took a sideways glance at Betty; the first of many as he kept the car thrusting south to the bright lights of London, still way out of view somewhere ahead.

Johnny peered in the rear-view mirror at Christine and then sideways at Betty. 'If I was just out looking for birds like you I'd be prepared, wouldn't I? I'd have a gun or a knife in the glovebox. Make out I was running out of petrol or something. Pull off the road, then threaten to kill Miss Stargazer back there unless you stripped off. What'd you say to that, darlin'? You'd have to be nice to me, whether you wanted it or not.'

'Don't talk like that. Please!' Betty's voice showed her uncertainty. Was he joking or not?

'I'm only giving it to you straight, Baby. You can forget this safety in numbers bit. It's a myth! There's some very funny blokes about these days. Very funny. And you can't tell us apart. You don't seem to realise that kids as dishy as you two - I mean, take that dress - leaves nothing to the imagination! Legs like you've got, darlin'! Sends 'em crazy for it, tongues hanging out. You're not just asking for it, you're screaming for it, far as they're concerned. Honest, I'm not kidding.'

'I'm glad you keep saying "them".' Betty wanted reassuring.

Johnny's smile seemed to do the trick. 'What's the trouble back home then? Or shouldn't I ask?'

Betty wished he hadn't. Christine had stopped listening. She was lost again in another world. She'd be no help in the explanation. Betty shot a sidelong glance at Johnny, her fingers fidgeting nervously with the strap of her handbag. After all, he was a complete stranger - yet somehow it seemed as if she'd know him all her life. He grinned at her.

Betty wondered how best to explain why they'd left home without going into the sordid business of all that had happened, not just tonight. The rows before their Mum ran away. The nights Dad came in boozed up. And the way he treated them like ten-year-olds, like anything except what they were, what they'd like to be if he'd only let them.

All right - she'd come in late tonight. Late by Dad's old-fashioned ideas. Nearly eleven o'clock, so what? She knew he'd be mad if he caught her. But chances were he'd gone to bed - he was on early shift, so she'd gambled on it. From the grimy soil in the tiny front garden she picked up a small stone and threw it at their bedroom window. It tapped lightly. She'd got good at it since she once cracked the pane, and was that a row - two days before he left off about it!

Quietly the old window frame slid up and Christine's hand dropped the key down. Betty opened the front door silently and took off her shoes on the mat. She closed the door but the hall wasn't quite dark because the moon streamed in through the frosted glass panel.

Betty just got one bare foot on the bottom stair. But no further. Ted Lane roared at her from the front room. 'You sneaking little bitch!'

She knew it was no use trying to argue and made a desperate dash for upstairs and the safety of a locked bedroom door. But Ted in a rage could spring nearly as fast as he could when he played goal for the Work's team. Beer and fags had slowed him and he'd let himself go for years. But in this fighting mood, he still jumped like a tiger. And he was on her before she'd reached the second stair.

Betty screamed. 'No, Dad. No! I've only been to the -' but he wasn't listening to excuses as he dragged her into the front room and pushed her down on the sofa. One big callused hand pressed hard into the nape of her neck, pinning her face down, her cries buried in the faded moquette. His other hand crashed heavy blows on to her skirt. But as he couldn't hear her screams, he flung up her skirt to belt her on her pants. But her young bottom was so clearly defined through her sheer tights that he reacted as if she were naked.

'You brazen little whore! Going out without pants on. All right! I'll make you bloody sorry you're not wearing good thick knickers.'

His temper was not quite uncontrollable. He grabbed at the top of her tights and ripped them down to the backs of her knees. With wild eyes never moving from his target, he flailed down in continuous strokes.

In the room above, Christine heard the sounds building up. Next door's dog added to the rumpus. She moved out onto the landing, and down the narrow staircase. She flung open the front door. Ted was still laying into Betty's slender body, nude and red-wealed from the waist down.

'I'll teach her to stay out on the streets till this hour. Once and for bloody all!'

Betty's protests were so distorted by her screams and struggles that Christine had to guess what she was saying. It sounded as if she'd only been to the flicks. That is exactly where she'd said she was going before she went out. Christine shouted at their father to stop.

Ted ceased, more from exhaustion than from taking any notice.

'Flicks were over an hour ago! Where've you been since then? Bad as your Mum. Little whores - both of you! You keep out of it, Christine or else I'll -'

He stopped mid-sentence as he looked at her transparent nightie - or rather, right through it.

He left Betty sobbing on the settee, made no attempt to pull her dress down, and bawled at her, as he surveyed Christine.

'Let that be a lesson to you, my girl. One you won't forget in a few days.'

Christine looked her father in the eye without wavering.

'You're a beast! Call yourself a father?'

Betty's voice became coherent. 'Chris! I didn't do anything! Honest! After the flicks we all went and had a coffee. We got talking and I'd no idea of the time and -'

Christine put her arm round Betty, still trembling and sobbing. She pushed her gently towards the hall.

'No use explaining. You can't argue with him. Go on up.'

Betty was glad to escape but Christine returned to the front room to have it out with him. He was wheezing after the exertion, his lungs labouring from years of chain-smoking. She'd seen him like this often before. Sometimes he'd put it on, trying to get sympathy. Bloody old hypocrite!

She stood in the doorway, pulling herself up to her full height. In spite of her youth, a figure of compelling dignity and power.

'If you lay as much as one finger on her again...'

'You'll...you'll what?' He could hardly get two words out together.

'Just don't ever touch her again, that's all.'

The different between his two daughters was never clearer to Ted Lane than at that moment. His anger began to rise again. He hadn't seen Christine in her new night-dress before. And he had not seen her unclothed since her mother had bathed the twins in front of the fire more than ten years ago.

It shocked him that his little daughter now had fully-formed breasts, that her figure was totally that of a woman's. But it came out quite differently.

'An' what d'you think you're doing? Going to bed dressed like a tart?'

'What are you calling me?' Her expression was icy. It infuriated him.

'You should be ashamed of yourself. You're as bad as she is. I've a good mind to teach you a lesson too.'

Anger recharged his energy and he grabbed at her. But Christine pulled away and the flimsy material tore in his hands. So he ripped it right down the front - a violent, angry gesture. Christine stood there, refusing to cover herself up, forcing him to face what he had done. Ted, embarrassed, looked away. Only then did she wrap the torn shreds across her breasts.

Christine's eyes burned hate at him.

'You've taught me a lesson all right. And I'll never forget it.' She walked out calmly - knowing now that she was in control of the situation. Ted followed, shouting, blustering.

'It's about time. You behave yourself - you and Betty - and dress decent. Stop parading your nakedness like that. I won't stand for it. Understand? Take note or you won't stay under this roof another night. I mean it.'

Christine turned on the tiny landing.

'You're dead right I won't. The sooner we're out of here the better - for both of us.'

Ted knew he couldn't make the staircase yet. He put all his effort into shouting: 'That's gratitude, isn't it? After all I've done. Bringing you up on my own. Father and mother to you. But I'm not surprised. I've seen it coming. I knew you were heading for trouble. Always thought you'd end up bad. Just like your Mum, you are, Christine. Just like her. Wilful. Bad, through and through.'

'Poor Mum! I can see what made her run off. Leaving you was the best thing she ever did. I wish I knew where she was now.'

Christine went into the bedroom and locked the door. Ted raged up the stairs after her but stopped half-way as his unhealthy condition caught up with him. He sank down, wheezing; a revolting sound.

'Don't...you talk...to me...like...' but the sentence ended with a groan.

Betty looked up at Christine from the huddle she made in the middle of her bed, sobbing and shaking.

'He was waiting for me - sitting there in the dark. He must have twigged that sometimes you drop me the key. Look where he grabbed me.'

She had scratches on her shoulders and arms. Christine was listening but not looking. She had pulled a large suitcase down from the rickety wardrobe and was putting her clothes in it, deliberately, calmly.

'What are you doing?'

'What does it look like?'

'I can see you're packing. I mean...what for?'

'I'm leaving.'

Christine began to take the drawing pins out of the glossy magazine cut-outs on the wall around her bed. They were all of fashion models; some showing off clothes, some with boyfriends and fast cars in lush places.

'But it's after midnight!'

'I don't care what time it is. I'm not staying in this dump with him. Not a minute longer!'

'Where'll you go?'

'London, of course,' Christine indicated the photographs as she put them on top of her folded clothes. 'Want to come?'

Betty gasped. 'How do we manage?'

Christine forestalled the question. She put her piggy bank on the bed. It stood fat and blue-patterned among the ruffled bed-clothes.

'How much in that, d'you think?'

'No idea - it's you money.'

'Fifty quid?'

'Much as that? No! Is there?' Betty's eyes widened in astonishment.

'Not far off, unless he's been at it. Let's see.'

Betty's mouth opened as Chris picked up the piggy and threw it as hard as she could onto the floorboards, just where the carpet strip was worn through. The piggy died instantly, its remains a jigsaw of jagged pot-pieces. From its stomach their key to freedom was delivered; fivers, ones, old-fashioned ten-bob notes, silver and a few three-penny pieces.

Christine gathered them up and stuffed them in her white handbag. 'About the only thing you can say for our Dad - he'd not a thief.'

'Fifty pounds! You've saved all that?'

'Near enough. It's been a long time coming, Betty. I've always meant it as something to see us through if this happened.'

'But you said you were saving up for your modelling course.'

'Same thing, isn't it? Except it'll be a London school, not a local one. Which is better, anyway.'

'But if we use it to live on, you won't have it for your course.'

Christine turned her large eyes on Betty.

'Have I ever let you down? Have I? Ever?'

'No, Chris, I don't mean that. I mean, it's all your cash, not half mine.'

'We'll work that out when the time comes.'

'Supposing Dad won't let us go.' Betty glanced nervously over her shoulder at the door, half afraid her father was lurking in readiness to strike again.

Christine's eyes narrowed.

'Try to stop us. He wouldn't dare.' She tiptoed to the door, flung it open as if to catch him listening. Nothing but the darkness of the landing met their gaze.

'He's going to suffer for what he did to us tonight.'

Christine was staring down, a strange fixed expression on her face. Betty felt a shiver go through her.

Ted was damping down the living-room fire for the night. He was still racked with the after-effects of his violence. He straightened up with difficulty, his face drawn, his breathing bad. He had a scared look as pain pierced his side and he held the palm of his hand hard against it as he reached the sideboard and pulled open another can of beer. He gulped from the can, spilled more than went down his throat, grunted at his own ineptitude. Worn out, he dropped into the armchair, grabbing at the threadbare arms for assistance. Then he turned his good ear to the ceiling, and listened. He thought he heard that loose board on the landing.

But it came from the staircase as Christine and Betty tiptoed down, holding their suitcases out in front of them so as not to bang them against the banisters.

Ted hauled himself up and walked heavily to the door. He opened it just as Christine was silently releasing the latch on the front door. For the first time Ted realised he had gone too far. 'I didn't say you had to go. You don't have to. Only if you don't behave better.'

'Goodbye, Dad.' Christine spoke for them both, with a calm finality.

'I'm not turning my little girls into the street. Never let that be said. Not of Ted Lane.' Maudlin now and a bit frightened.

'No - you're not turning us out. We're leaving of our own accord.' Christine was adamant.

'I was only doing it for your own good. Honest!' His breathing was more difficult as the emotion welled up. 'Chris, Betty - please!'

He held out his coarse hands. Christine put her arm round Betty as she shrank from him. 'No, Dad. Chris, stop him!'

'I'm not going to hurt you. You've taken your punishment. It's over. Let's forget it. Wipe the slate clean. Start again.'

'Until next time!' Christine was scornful. She gave her sister a little shove through the door.

'Go on, Betty.'

Betty hesitated, looking back at her father.

'Dad, we're going because...well, we can't stand any more.'

Ted's face was putty-coloured, his breath rasping. 'Please...'
His mouth worked but no sounds came out.

Christine smiled coolly. 'You can take it you are driving us
out if you like. Doesn't much matter either way.'

He leaned against the door frame, made a big effort.

'Look kids, you're my only children. All I have. You know
I've not been well. You can't leave me alone -'

Christine cut him off without mercy.

'Don't come that sob-stuff with us. We know you too well!'

'I can't get my breath. Honest! I'm not putting it on. I really
can't.'

Christine pushed Betty out and followed her.

'Oh, get lost!' were the last words she ever said to him. She
slammed the door so hard in his pleading face it reverberated
down the street, where eyes peered through curtains and ears
strained in unlit rooms.

Ted reeled and clutched at the banister, fighting to fill his lungs
with clean air. The pain in his side spread, engulfing him in a
speechless agony until unconsciousness came as a blessing.

How much, Betty wondered as they sped through the night, how much of all that sordid business did you tell anyone? Why go into all the details? Why explain? Especially to a complete stranger who was giving you a lift. It might give him the wrong idea about you. So she settled for brevity. What was the trouble back home? She summed it up in two words. 'Dad, mostly.'

'Oh. The generation gap, eh?' Johnny sounded sympathetic.

'Didn't speak the same language. He was so old-fashioned you wouldn't believe it! Rules and regulations out of the Ark. Don't do this, don't do that. We couldn't move without causing a row. It was impossible.'

'I know the type, darlin'.' Johnny's voice grew mockingly stern. 'Now girls, I'm not stopping you going out and enjoying yourselves. But you'll be back in this house at ten sharp - or there'll be ructions. And no boyfriend in the porch or he'll get my boot up his backside. Understand?'

Betty giggled. 'That's not far off our Dad, is it, Chris?'

Christine looked at the curly hair at the back of Johnny's head. 'Anyway, there's no life for anyone in the provinces.'

'That right?' Johnny wasn't asking, just drawing them out.

'Not if you want to be someone, get somewhere.' Christine's tone indicated that she certainly intended to.

'And you do, of course?' Johnny wanted to hear more.

'Why not? When you read what goes on in London, it only makes you green. We're going where the action is.'

Johnny glanced at her in his rear-view mirror. 'Don't blame me if you're disappointed when you've had some of it.'

'You know it well, don't you?' asked Betty.

'Cockney. Born and bred. Proud of it.'

Christine ran her long nails along the leather seat-arm.

'We won't be disappointed. You must be doing all right. With a car like this.'

'Would be, wouldn't I, if it was mine.'

Betty looked at him as if he had stolen it.

'Isn't it yours, then?'

Johnny smiled wryly.

'Good as, I use it whenever I want it.'

'What's that mean - good as? It doesn't really belong to you then?'

Johnny nodded. She suspected a bloke like him had no right to be driving such a super car.

'You're dead right, darlin'. It doesn't belong to me at all.'

'Whose is it?'

'One of our clients - my best client, in fact. I'm in the trade. Always know where you can put your hand on a nice clean motor car. Particularly something a bit special. New - second-hand - you name it. And this particular client likes to change motors as often as you've had hot dinners. Been happy with this one longer than ten or twelve others before it. Must have had it all of five weeks now.'

'And you drive it wherever you want to?'

'Well, I look after it too, see. Keep it in top nick. All that jazz. I have to give it road tests, don't I? No one minds what I do so long as I drop it there where it's wanted. And it looks good and it goes good.'

'How marvellous! Fancy having a car like this for nothing.'

'Not for nothing, darlin'. I get paid for it. Handsomely. I told you - my best client easily.'

Betty's eyes showed her admiration for Johnny. She was glad he hadn't pretended it was his car. He could have done so.

'I'd die if I owned a car like this. I really would.'

'You never know. You might hit the jackpot in London. Some streets are still paved with gold - so they say. I've never found 'em. Got something to go to, have you? Relations? A job?'

'Well, not exactly. Chris and I decided - well, it was her idea really - that we'd just go. We'll find somewhere to live when we get there. Then start looking around. You know?'

'Show business? That idea?' His eyes looked down, mocking her. She tossed her head.

'Don't be silly. What makes you say that?'

'Coupla good lookers. That's all it takes to start with.'

'How d'you mean?'

'Well, they don't make singers and actresses out of bow-legged, cross-eyed birds, do they?'

'Thanks for the compliment. What do you know about it?'

'Well, I know that much. I get around.'

'Bet you do.'

'No, honest. You're a little smasher. Some birds look all

right you know - eyes and hair and all that, till you look at their legs. I mean you've either got good legs or you haven't. There's nothing you can do about it.'

'So you've been looking at my legs?' Betty was beginning to talk more easily to Johnny.

'Course! You show enough of 'em. What for? Not to make me look the other way, I bet. Then you get birds with legs like yours and a chest like a billiard table. But you -' He whistled his appreciation.

Betty was flattered but pretended not to be.

'Christine's the one with the looks. She won a beauty competition. Only local but still -'

Johnny checked in the rear-view mirror again.

'That figures. With that figure!' He chuckled at the pun.

Christine explained briefly.

'One beauty competition was enough. Thanks very much! I'm for better things than cattle-shows.'

'She's going to be a model.' Betty's enthusiasm bubbled up and Johnny suppressed the groan that the words automatically evoked.

'That's a tough old racket!'

Christine was listening, but still watching the world flash by in the moonlight.

'Not if you go into it properly. I'm going to take a course. Learn the job from scratch.'

'That's all right then. So long as you've got the loot and go to a reputable agency. There are some shockers, I warn you. Don't get mixed up with any of them photographers. You know - the back-street boys. The sort that advertises in newsagents' windows. They'll whisper all sorts of promises in your ear. The earth. Know what I mean?'

Christine turned from the window at last and smiled knowingly.

'Give you the earth and it turns out to be the dirt.'

'Very good. Like that. Not bad. Yeah, they'll do you dirt all right, those boys. And make you pay good money for the privilege, like as not!'

Betty was not the same wary girl who got in the car.

'We know what we're doing. We won't get caught as easily as that.'

Johnny gave quick searching glance at Betty. Her in the

back, she knew how many beans made five. But he wasn't sure about this one, the one he fancied.

'Come to think of it, I know one or two places where they've got rooms. My Mum lets out bedsitters. Any use? I could drop you round there, you could have a look see. Okay?'

Betty liked the idea.

'Oh yes, that would be -'

Suddenly Christine leapt forward from the back seat.

'Look out!'

Her hand gripped Johnny's shoulders and instinctively he did his Jackie Stewart thing. The Jaguar screeched in protest but obediently slewed to the right without slowing down. And only as it did so could Johnny see how nearly they had missed disaster. How nearly they could all have been killed. Just discernible in the headlights as they flashed by, was a small dark car being pushed along by two men. The car hand no lights. The men were in dark evening-suits.

Not realising how near they'd been to death, too, the men angrily waved and shouted curses. But the Jag had left them far behind in a matter of seconds.

Betty still hand her hand to her mouth. Johnny whistled with relief. Christine leaned back again, calm and composed.

'Blimey, you must be able to see in the dark.'

'She can, can't you, Chris? I call her Cat Eyes.'

Johnny looked at Chris in the mirror. Did her large eyes glow luminously? Or was it a trick of the lights from the dashboard? He concentrated on the road a little harder.

Some minutes later the night began to give way to the dawn. Johnny looked at his watch.

'There's a phone box on the corner of a lane somewhere near here, I've used it before. This next one, I think. Yes. I want to call my boss; report I'm on my way in.'

He turned into a hedgerowed lane and drove past the box, round a bend until it was out of sight.

As he pulled on the hand-brake, he saw Betty's apprehensive eyes, taking in the overhanging trees, hearing no signs of life except for the early morning bird-song.

'Don't worry, I'm not going to rape you,' he joked.

Christine was scornful. 'You bet you're not.'

Betty smiled wanly. 'I wasn't thinking that.' But it was crossing her mind, if she admitted the truth.

'It's the sort of lonely place a bloke might bring a bird if he meant business - I mean dirty business.'

Johnny leaned ominously across Betty, making her feel she was pinned back into her seat by his arm. He opened the glove box, watching her eyes concentrating on what he was taking out. He smiled, waving a notepad under her nose. 'Just in case the boss has an address for me to drive straight to from here.' He smiled mischievously.

Christine did not think it was funny.

'That was a cheap trick. You frightened her.'

'No, he didn't, Chris. Honest.'

Johnny looked at Betty. 'It's worth it, if she remembers the lesson.' Then with a cheeky grin he set off back to the telephone box.

Betty watched him go. 'He wouldn't hurt a fly. I think he's sweet.'

'It could still be a big act. To take us in.'

'I don't believe it.'

Christine shrugged. 'Okay - but you must admit it's a funny old time to make a phone call. I'm going to spend a penny. Coming?' She surveyed the thick vegetation.

'No, I'm all right.'

Christine walked away from the car looking for a gap to get through the hedge. She saw one back in the direction Johnny had taken. But as she reached it, the telephone box caught her eye. It was empty. And Johnny wasn't in sight anywhere. She frowned. That was funny. But having more urgent things to do, she went through the gap.

In the car Betty turned on the radio. Early morning get-up-and-go-to-work-with-a-beat music banged out. She flicked her fingers, her whole body beating four-to-the-bar.

Christine had taken advantage of a small clearing encircled by undergrowth. She felt better as she ran her hands up her legs, smothering her tights to take up the slack. She held her skirts waist-high to check there was no ripple to spoil the line of her legs. She stood still for a moment, appreciating how lucky she was to be so well endowed. As Johnny said, you had good legs or you hadn't. If you had, show them off the best you could, that was her motto.

She froze as she heard a rustle in the greenery behind her. She dropped her skirt subconsciously as she listened. Then she tiptoed through the dewy grass in the direction of the sound. She pulled aside a leaf-laden branch and her cheek muscles tightened. There was Johnny and he was acting very strangely.

He was looking at a piece of twig, stuck in the ground, one branch of it pointing horizontally. He took a gold identity-chain from his wrist. He measured out the length of the chain five times from the twig, exactly in the direction the branch was sign-posting.

At this precisely located point he scraped away the lose earth with his hand and pulled a small package from its tiny grave. He pocketed it; and refastened the bracelet on his wrist. Christine tiptoed quietly but hurriedly back through the gap in the hedge.

Betty was still swinging to the music when Christine reached the car, breathless from her run along the lane. She turned off the radio.

'Betty! D'you know what I've just seen?'

Before she could say any more, Johnny came innocently into view.

'I'll have to tell you later.' Christine silently indicated not in front of Johnny. Betty was intrigued.

As the Jaguar's snub head thrust down the main road to London again, Christine acted as though nothing had happened. She started a new conversation casually enough.

'I expect you get about a lot in your job?'

'That's one of the things I like about it. Going place. Meeting all kinds of people.' He offered Betty a cigarette pack. She refused but Christine took one when he held it over his shoulder.

Christine pretended to see the gold bracelet for the first time. She slipped her finger through it and hung on.

'That's nice,' she said admiringly. 'Real gold?'

'Birthday present.' Johnny pulled his hand away. It might have been that he needed it on the wheel. Christine wasn't sure.

Betty challenged him. 'From your wife? Or a girlfriend?'

'Neither! Do I look the marrying type? And I'm not

19

attached elsewhere at present...' He laughed at the thought.

Christine was naturally suspicious.

'Don't tell me it's from a man.'

'Do you mind? I've been called some things in my mind, but never that.'

Christine pressed. 'Well, if it's not from a girl it must be a man.'

Johnny was puzzled. 'I didn't say it wasn't from a girl!'

'Yes you did. Only a wife or girlfriend would give you a present like that.'

'If you must know, it's from a client.'

Christine's comment sounded suspicious. 'You do all right from some of your clients, don't you?'

'It's the same one that owns this wagon. She's very generous.'

'She?' Betty fastened on the word. 'Your best client is a woman, then?'

'Nothing strange in that. She's Abby Drake. You've probably heard of her.'

'Abby Drake, the singer? In the charts a few weeks back?' Betty was immediately interested.

'That's her. Anything to do with cars, she asks me. And she pays well.'

'I liked her last single.' Betty was the pop fan in the Lane family. 'We were always playing it at our Club.'

Christine elaborated for Johnny's benefit. 'Our Youth Club runs a discotheque at weekends. Betty lived with that pile of records.'

'D'you blame me? It was the only place really going, back home. You know Abby Drake well? Lucky you.'

Johnny pinched some of the star's glory. 'Abby's cut more discs than you've had hot dinners.' He said it as if it was partly due to his association with her.

Christine jibed straight back. 'You do stand up for her don't you? Quite a nice little set-up you're on to, seems to me.'

Johnny nearly turned round in spite of the Jag's speed. 'Now look do you want to see these rooms or not? Because if you do, cut out the snide remarks, see?'

Betty was in quickly. 'Yes, please. We do!'

'Then let's have a bit more respect for my boss. She can sing. That's more than you can say for most of 'em.'

Christine realised Johnny's offer might be useful.

'We didn't suggest she couldn't. I like Abby Drake. Really.'

Betty added weight: 'And Chris is pretty choosy, I can tell you.'

'All right then. Mind, I'm not talking about Buckingham Palace.'

Betty chuckled. 'That's not what we're used to, exactly.'

Johnny smiled back. 'She's Chris. What's your name?'

'Haven't we said? Oh, I'm Betty. Betty Lane. What's yours?'

It was quite a large room, with two divan beds. Although the window looked out towards one of the larger London parks, it wasn't Buckingham Palace for sure. The twins had unpacked. Betty was working on a shopping list. Christine was more concerned with her fashion gallery, pinning her cut-outs to the wall in the same pattern that she had displayed back home.

Betty's brow was furrowed. 'Can't think of anything else we'll need. For the next few days anyway. Oh, we must start collecting shillings for the meter.'

Christine reached up to pin the corners of a large photograph of a girl in the briefest bikini. The background was a golden beach and Italianate sky. But Christine's own limbs, revealed by the long stretch, were quite as gorgeous as those of the model.

Betty didn't notice, of course.

'Hope we get jobs before the money runs out, that's all.' She sounded doubtful.

'Have I ever let you down, Betty? I've promised you we'll be all right.' Christine stood back to admire her hanging. Hotchpotch though her fashion gallery was, it was an improvement on the faded wallpaper - the only pattern now discernible was in damp marks.

'Chris, we are lucky! Getting a room like this right off. First go, I mean.'

'It'll do for the time being.'

'We could have been tramping round for ages if it hadn't been for Johnny.'

Christine swung her gaze from her pictures to get Betty's reaction to her question.

'You haven't fallen for him, have you?'

'Don't be ridiculous! I hardly know him.'

Christine smiled. She could read her sister like a book. Of course the little idiot had fallen for him - and in a big way. So what? Why should Christine mind.

Betty got the message. 'Well, what if I have then? I've never met anyone as nice as him. He's been so kind and helpful. You must admit that.'

Christine pulled an expression of doubt. She still hadn't

brought herself to mention the bracelet episode. She didn't know why. Maybe because she didn't really know what to make of it. Or she didn't want to scare Betty. The kid was so excited - no point in stirring things up until she was more certain of the facts. She was amused to catch herself once again thinking of her sister as a kid.

'Watch him. Be careful. I've a feeling he's a sharp character.'

'What makes you say that? Just because he talks quick, and catches on fast? That's nothing to go by.'

'Of course not, silly. Come on.' Christine took her arm. 'If we spend all day talking about Johnny Dixon, we'll never find a job.'

The newsagent's board was the very type that Johnny had warned them about. But there they were, both with the giggles, reading the cards out to each other.

Christine's finger pointed. '"Lady will share bed and breakfast". She's got a nerve!'

Betty could hardly believe the next one. '"Miss Stern. Discipline given". I've got a good idea what that means. How can they do it?' She made a grimace of distaste.

Christine was enjoying herself.

'Look at this! - "Model with good figure, for photographers. Camera supplied if requested".'

Betty found the joke wearing thin and tugged at Christine.

'We won't find anything here. They're just what Johnny told us about.'

'I know. But it's a laugh isn't it? Look, Betty, you try the Labour Exchange. For us both, I mean.'

'What are you going to do?'

'I'll tell you later. See you back at the digs!'

Betty was a bit chary but agreed. It was Christine's smile - as usual.

'All right. Don't do anything I wouldn't do.'

They parted, laughing. Being in London on their own, being able to decide exactly what they wanted to do next and do it - this was living. And they'd never known such freedom in their lives before.

Freedom to do what was a question they didn't ask themselves.

Christine watched Betty wave as she disappeared round a corner. She waved back. Then her arm dropped and she turned to the newsagent's window, drawn by something she had seen earlier. Not on the noticeboard, but amongst the displayed magazines. An attractive woman's face, with strong features and magnetic eyes, stared at her. She read the caption: 'Sybil Waite. Wizard of commercial photography, pictured here in her studio. Miss Waite has been responsible for discovering some of the most successful and beautiful models.'

The newsagent was busy selling the day's papers. His regular customers queued up, paid, took their regular orders and moved on with hardly a word passing. He noticed Christine standing transfixed, staring, it would seem, at his displayed stock. In a momentary break he snapped: 'Yes, Miss?' She didn't hear him.

She picked up the magazine and flicked through it. In the centre pages there was a double page spread feature dominated by a colour picture of Sybil Waite at her mahogany desk. The caption read: 'Miss Waite has a flair for discovering beautiful girls. She has a long list of successful models to her credit. On these pages are pictures of just a few of them.'

The newsagent was too busy to do more than glance reprovingly at Christine, as she flicked through Sybil Waite's stable of lovelies. She was oblivious of him, until he got another moment to bark: 'Three and six, dear, please.'

Christine handed him the money without looking away from the pictures. As he took it he couldn't resist cracking: 'In the modelling game yourself then, are you?'

'Yes, I am, as a matter of fact. What's my quickest way to the King's Road from here?'

It wasn't a very large sign which indicated Sybil Waite's Studio at the better end of King's Road. You might have missed it, unless you knew the street number. But it was beautifully painted, artistic and shouting good taste. Christine didn't miss it. She passed under it, through the open door and straight up the white stairs as the arrow indicated. In any case, all she had to do was follow the bevy of beautiful girls, framed professional photographs of Sybil Waite's models lining the staircase. She examined them eagerly and became more and more impressed. By the time she reached the door marked Reception just a little of her confidence had been sapped.

But she didn't hesitate to knock. A female voice said 'Come in' sharply. And when Christine opened the door she saw it belonged to a middle-aged dragon, glaring at her through heavy, dark-framed spectacles. A smartly dressed dragon nevertheless.

'Yes?' she asked sharply.

'I'd like to see Miss Waite.'

'What's your name?'

'Lane. Christine Lane.'

The room was entirely decorated in shades of blue; walls, ceiling, woodwork, furniture, curtains, carpet. Christine noted what an artistic effect it created. She'd never seen an office like it before.

The Receptionist hardly glanced at her desk diary. 'Miss Waite has no appointment booked for you. Sorry.' She didn't sound the least bit sorry. She implied that it was the end of the conversation and that Christine should leave immediately.

'I've travelled a long way. I've only just arrived in London. I've come specially to see her.' Christine clutched at straws.

'Miss Waite can't possibly see you, wherever you've come from. She's out.'

'Oh...I only wanted a minute. Just to ask her advice, that's all...'

'If she stopped to give advice to every girl that came to this office she'd never have any time at all for work.'

'Then could you tell me how I get to see her? How all those girls up the staircase...'

'You'd better write in. Send a composite if you've got one.' The snooty tone of voice implied that she was certain Christine hadn't got one, even if she knew what it was.

'I'll try to fit you in at the end of the week.'

'But it's very urgent.'

'Look Miss...Lane, when I say she's not in, she's not in. To you or anyone.'

Christine's eyes had become increasingly attracted to a door behind the Reception Desk marked with the one word, Private. Now she couldn't take her eyes off it for some unaccountable reason.

'I see. Then I'll wait.'

And she sat on the sofa, her gaze fixed on the door. The dragon sighed impatiently. What a difficult girl this was. But the most aspiring models were difficult. And Miss Fletcher had dealt with countless numbers in her time.

'Now look, I've told you! It won't do any good.'

At that moment the Private door opened and Sybil Waite came out. Christine recognised her from the magazine and jumped up, unable to control her excitement.

It was as if a famous actress had made her first carefully rehearsed entrance. But Sybil Waite, without seeming to do anything other than opening the door to say something quite ordinary, created a magnetic effect on Christine. She looked smart, that was to be expected. But it seemed to have been achieved without all the trouble Christine went to when she wanted to look really stunning.

Miss Waite's dress was simple; it was expensive material, she could tell that. Wow! Those shoes must have cost her a bomb. Only one piece of jewellery, a brooch that probably cost even more. Her hair looked as though she'd just whisked a comb through it. Bet she hadn't though, thought Christine. She'd been to that top man who was always in the papers.

Sybil Waite began talking to Miss Fletcher the moment she came out. As if Christine were not there. Her voice was low, yet incisive. Christine did not really follow what she was talking about, but she listened to every word.

'Chase up Pollons for the soap proofs, Fletch. They should have been here an hour ago. Promised faithfully, by Howard himself. What's he doing, having a baby or something? Wouldn't surprise me, come to think of it.'

Christine smiled, though nobody noticed.

'Yes, right away.' Miss Fletcher was as servile as she was superior only a moment ago.

Christine found herself saying: 'Miss Waite?'

Sybil turned slowly.

There was an immediate impact as their eyes met. Each of them only half heard Fletch justifying her job.

'I did explain that you're busy. But she insisted on waiting.'

Christine didn't take her eyes from Sybil's.

'Could you please spare me five minutes? Just five. Please!'

Sybil was the first to break the spell. She looked at her gold watch. She hesitated, then: 'I'll give you two.'

'Oh thank you, Miss Waite. It's very good of -'

Sybil ignored the gratitude and turned to her secretary. 'Fletch, book me a cab for lunch...' She looked Christine up and down, from hair to shoes and back again, not missing anything on the way. Christine waited for her favourable reaction.

'I don't think I'll be long.' That meant more than two minutes, anyway, Christine hoped.

Sybil turned into her office. Fletch, annoyed at Christine for getting past her, snapped: 'Well, go on! Miss Waite hasn't got all day.'

Christine needed no second command and was through the door, gladly suffering Fletch's scowl until it closed behind her.

If the Reception's all-blue effect had an impact of Christine, it was nothing to her reaction to the Studio. Much of it was unlit. The rest was in pools of light directed from hard-focus spotlights into key areas. Miss Waite's big desk was in the biggest light spot. Behind it there was a huge blow-up of two nude girls facing each other. A mosaic of Sybil Waite lovelies decorated the opposite wall, and a set of six long frames displayed leggy models, provocatively undressed and revealing.

Walls, floor and ceiling were all black, and it was difficult to discern the true size of the room.

'Come along. Stand where I can see you.'

Sybil, almost in silhouette from back lighting, was behind her desk, indicating Christine should stand in front of her. Christine moved in to the spotlight. Sybil flicked a switch, and doubled the light intensity on that small area. Christine's confidence practically drained away. She felt she was under a microscope.

'I presume you want to be a model?'

Christine explained eagerly: 'Yes. But I'm not just saying that. I know it won't be easy. I've saved up for a course. All I want to ask you...well, I can't expect to start at the top, I mean with someone famous like you...so, could you tell me that best place to try. For a girl just beginning?'

Christine could tell from the way the dark outline of Sybil was so still and from the long pause before she replied that she was looking at her very hard.

Christine firmly squashed a sudden desire that all the lights would go out and door marked Private would open so that she could rush out.

'If you could get the odd photographic job or two meanwhile. It would help to pay your way?'

Christine could hardly believe her ears.

'Oh, yes, if I could! Only I don't really know how to go about it.'

Sybil had taken a form from the top drawer of her desk while the girl was speaking. Now she began to fill in the blanks, looking at Christine for the answers as she worked down the paper.

Christine looked at the photographs behind Sybil. She'd never seen such lovely girls. No wonder they didn't mind being photographed nude. They had something to show off, to be proud of. She felt she had too, but it probably took a bit of nerve to do it all the same. Different from showing off beautiful clothes, although you needed a good figure for that also. Christine knew - she just knew - she could wear clothes well, given the chance. That's all she wanted, the chance.

Sybil did not seem so certain.

'Mmmm,' she murmured. Christine could almost hear her two allotted minutes ticking away. As if some clanging alarm bell would remind Sybil her time was up at any moment.

'Mmmm. Difficult.' Sybil seemed to be talking to herself, as if Christine were not there. Then at last she looked up and spoke to her.

'Still...you're an attractive girl. You should photograph well. What's your name?'

'Christine Lane.'

'Christina.'

'No. Not Christina. Christine.' She stressed the last syllable, believing her pronunciation was at fault.

'I prefer Christina. For a girl like you. I have a feeling about names.'

There was no argument. Anyway, Christine didn't want one.

No point in risking her luck.

'Right Christina. First thing to get clear is this. There's very little fun and glamour in this business. It's damned hard work. You understand that?'

'Oh yes. I'm prepared to work very hard. I'll do anything I'm told.'

She meant it. But it provoked a searching glance from Sybil.

'Will you? Without question, without complaining?'

'Of course. I'm used to working for my living.'

'How about nudes?'

Christine's eyes flashed to the girl's highlit nakedness behind Sybil. Her mouth dropped a little. But she didn't say anything. After all, it was not as if she hadn't half expected it. She'd just have to get used to the idea - it was part of the job. That was the way to look at it. Her mouth was dry, as Sybil carried on, business-like and casual. Somehow her professional attitude made the prospect easier.

'There's a big demand for nudes these days. And it's growing. There isn't a single product on the market that can't be sold with a naked girl. Incredible, isn't it?'

'I was hoping to do fashion...that sort of job. Well, you hear about these back-street photographers...'

Sybil looked straight at her with a reassuring smile.

'My dear girl, we're not talking about nudies. Get that right out of your mind. This is a professional organisation. I wouldn't send you to one of those rat-bag studios. Good heavens! Little more than legalised brothels, some of them. You must steer clear of that lot. I'm just wondering...' She tapped the gold pen against her teeth thoughtfully. 'I'm just wondering...'

So was Christine. Her original two minutes had to be up. Easily.

'I'm wondering if I could do something for you myself. You see, the commercial nude is an easier way of breaking in, no doubt about that. Particularly if you're young, just fully-formed, you know what I mean. I could tell you some very big names who were only too happy for the chance. Couldn't wait to get their clothes off. Of course, they don't like to be reminded of it. Now they play very hard to get before they strip to the buff. But they still do it if the money's right. Once the first embarrassment wears off, they parade their breasts

and bottoms with the same aplomb they give to a five-thou-
sand-guinea fur coat.'

'You think, after a while, it's...easy?'

'I should know dear,' Sybil vaguely indicated the mural display.

'Oh, I'm not doubting you. I suppose it makes sense.'

'Well then, let's have a look at you, shall we? See what
you're made of. Undress over there.'

Sybil waved towards a black chair. Christine noted with relief
that it was in the shadows and moved to it, glad to get out of the
hard light where she had felt herself under such close inspection.
She had to summon all her youthful bravado to go through with
this. Funny how nervous she felt all of a sudden. It wasn't so
much the thought of stripping - she knew her figure was every bit
as good as the models on the wall... No - it was something about
Sybil that made Christine feel unsure of herself. A quick glance
reassured her that the older woman was now seated at her desk,
scrutinising papers, signing, not looking up at all, taking it for
granted she was getting undressed.

Christine made a sudden decision. She reminded herself that
this was the chance she'd been longing for all these months.
And it had come sooner than she could possibly have hoped.
Ridiculous to ruin it now because of a last minute fit of
nerves. She put her hand up to her neck and quickly unzipped
her dress and let it fall to the ground. Nothing like jumping in
at the deep end.

Sybil put her hand under her desk. Was it Christine's imagination or was the level of light coming up, like theatre lights
did, very gradually? It didn't seem quite so dim. Or maybe her
eyes were getting used to it. Sybil glanced up for a second,
saw Christine was still in bra and pants.

'Don't be long, dear. My cab will be here.' Her voice was
matter-of-fact, consciously so.

Christine reached for the bra fastening. She paused just for a
moment, her eyes on Sybil who seemed unconcerned, eyes
down, her mind on her work. Christine slipped the fastening,
holding both ends in the centre of her back.

Sybil's papers were lit by a student lamp fashioned in high-
ly-polished brass. In its reflection she watched Christine take
her bra straps under her arms. Her breasts were firm even

when she slipped off the shoulder straps. Sybil turned over a paper mechanically as if she had read it, but her eyes never left the reflection.

Christine began to feel as though she were getting undressed at bedtime. After all, Betty was usually there and she didn't watch her either. Sybil could hardly prevent herself taking a direct look. But she knew from past experience that a young girl stripping for the first time could still take fright even at this juncture. This one must not. She dared not risk it.

Christine put her thumbs in her tights but froze as Sybil asked: 'Do you have any photographs?'

She still did not look up from her papers.

Christine's mouth was still dry as she answered.

'No, I'm afraid I haven't.'

'You'll need some.'

Christine pulled her tights down over her thighs. As her legs lost their sheath they looked even more attractive. She had always found this as she undressed and it helped her today.

'What have I got to hide,' she told herself, convincingly.

Sybil was making a note on her pad.

'I'll see if I can get one of my boys to do some for you on the cheap.'

'Oh thank you.'

Christine was now naked, and trembling almost imperceptibly. It wasn't cold, quite warm with the lights, but she stayed near the chair, not quite certain what to do.

'Well, are we ready?' Sybil sounded almost like that doctor who had examined her. Of course in those days she was only just beginning to notice her own breasts. It was a few years ago, now. But the clinical tone gave her confidence and she adopted what she considered a model stance, hand on hip, head tossed back a little.

'You're not cold, are you?' Sybil flicked another switch and the light Christine thought had brightened a bit came up fully. It seemed such a harsh light, making her skin pale and her hair glisten. It shone directly in her eyes and she couldn't see where Sybil was. From the sound of her voice she had left her desk and was standing very close in the immediate darkness.

'No. I'm just a little...nervous.' Christine was more ashamed of her embarrassment than her nakedness.

There was a long silence which she found almost more unnerving. Sybil Waite must have been very close. She could actually hear her breathing. Then came her voice, quiet almost down to a whisper.

'Yes, not bad. Quite good breasts in fact. I do like to see character in breasts. They should assert themselves, like yours do. A tip for you dear. Splash them with lemon juice just before a photograph. Legs are good, too. Thighs not too heavy, just right. Turn round; let me see your bottom.'

In a way turning round seemed to make Christine feel more vulnerable. Hearing someone talk so clinically about her body was a strange experience - but there was more than just an interview here.

'Yes, that's good too. Nice arch to the small of the back.' And Christine felt Sybil's hand stroke her gently in that area. Just to indicate where she meant?

'Very important you go in there, dear.' Her hand was taken away. 'And a good bottom. Not too big. Big bottoms are death. Watch your bottom, Christina, it's many a girl's downfall. To the side on, please.'

Obedient, Christine turned as instructed. Out of the corner of her eye she saw Sybil bend forward to run her eye along the line of her bosom. Her hand came up as if she were about to touch Christine. Christine went cold. So this was it! But just at that moment, a buzzer sounded and Sybil moved back to the desk. Her attitude was casual, matter-of-fact as she talked to Miss Fletcher on the intercom.

'Thank you. Tell the driver to wait. I shan't be long.'

Christine stared at her. This was the crunch. Did she get dressed and walk out of this studio right away? Or should she stay, knowing full well what could happen? She was surprised to find herself quite calm now, assembling her thoughts and viewing the situation in a strictly calculated way. How much did she want this modelling career? More than anything in the world, that was for sure. Definite. Whatever the cost.

Sybil looked at Christine again.

'Now where were we? Oh yes.' Sybil picked up a tape measure and came very close to her. They stood face to face.

Christine returned her stare, far more confident now that her mind was made up and the course of action decided. Sybil held out the tape measure.

'Lift your arms, please.' Sybil encircled her bust with the tape.

'Thirty-five.' The words were Christine's.

'Thirty-five is right. But you'd be surprised at the figures some girls give. My records have to be accurate. So I check them personally. Now the waist.'

'Twenty-two,' Sybil this time.

Christine asked deliberately: 'Will you be able to do anything for me, Miss Waite?'

The measure was lowered to her thighs. Sybil was avoiding looking at her.

'I may be able to - thirty-four - if you promise to be guided by me.'

'Of course!' Funny how calm she felt now, almost in control, as if she had the power over Sybil in a way.

'No "of course" about it, Christina. Girls will say anything at this stage just to get me to take them on. But you'd be surprised how many of them forget - and quickly too. It's discipline I require. Obedience without question.'

'I understand, Miss Waite...You won't have any trouble with me.' There was a different tone in the girl's voice and Sybil shot a sharp glance up at her. Christine smile back blandly.

Sybil took a final lingering look as she said: 'All right you can get dressed now.'

Christine went to her clothes and started to pull on her panties. Sybil noted down the measurements on the form and reached for a secret button under her desk. It buzzed another telephone, a red one this time. She pretended to answer it and carried on a conversation, checking from time to time that Christine was listening. The telephone wires ran under the desk one as far as the buzz button. It was connected to nowhere.

'Hello...Yes, Peter, love, what can I do for you?'

She paused to give time for the imaginary caller to answer, her eyes watching Christine cupping her breasts in her bra.

'Tomorrow? You have to be joking! Are they out of their tiny minds? I know it's a big job. And they're very good clients... But where am I going to find the right girl between now and tomorrow? All the models worth having were booked up weeks ago.' She paused and sighed at the enormity of the problem. 'Well, I'll work out something.' She paused again. 'Don't worry. I'll find the right girl, even if I have to take her off some other job...Yes, I promise.' Pause. 'Yes, we can use Wychwold. I'll fix it with Gerald. Ring me later and I'll tell you what I've dreamed up. Bye.' She replaced the fake telephone.

'Some people expect miracles!' She glanced across and saw that Christine was dressed. 'That's quick! Quicker than you peeled them off!'

'Miss Waite, I couldn't help hearing -'

'Nothing confidential, my dear.'

'No, I mean...would I be suitable?'

'Suitable for what?' Sybil was playing it very cool. She scanned through the papers in an abstract way.

'For the job. The one you were talking about on the phone just now.'

Sybil smiled tolerantly. 'My dear child, it's a tricky assignment. One of our biggest accounts. It needs someone with a lot of experience.'

Christine did not disguise her eagerness. 'I learn fast. Everyone says that. You'd only have to tell me once. And I don't mind how hard I work!'

'That's all very well, but... No, it's too big a risk.'

Christine instinctively felt that she had to the advantage now. 'Oh, please! Please, Miss Waite. I won't let you down. I know I won't!'

Sybil paused, acting undecided, giving Christine the impression she was being talked into it. 'It would mean working over the weekend.' A meaningful pause. 'In the country.'

'I don't mind. I'm not doing anything.'

'We're going to use a gorgeous house. Owned by a friend of mine. Perfect for this sort of ad. Lovely backgrounds.'

'I wouldn't care if it were a coal mine. Give me a chance, please.'

'Well...' She seemed doubtful. 'I'll think about it.' She picked up an embossed visiting card from the desk and handed it to Christine. 'Ring me later. About four-thirty. If I haven't found anyone suitable by then, I might take a chance on you.'

Christine made for the door, looking at the card.

'Four-thirty. I'll ring on the dot.'

'You haven't got the job yet. Don't count your chickens.'

But Christine was sure she had. 'Thank you, Miss Waite. You won't regret this, I promise!' And she waltzed past Miss Fletcher and down the stairs in a whirl of elation and triumph.

Fletch went into the Studio. Sybil was dialling a number and whilst waiting for the answer, she unconsciously stroked a paperweight. It was a coiled snake, its head raised to strike. She smiled and handed Fletch the form headed 'Christina Lane'.

'When she rings at four-thirty, keep her waiting before putting her through.'

❛ Johnny - no!' Betty pleaded urgently.

'Don't stop me now! Have a heart!'

After all, Betty had invited him in and she hadn't minded when he drew the curtains and pulled her down on to the bed. He certainly hadn't imagined her eager response to his kissing. Now she gripped his wrist, trying to force him to stop.

'Johnny, I said no.'

Johnny did not believe that she really meant 'No' and started to tug at her panties. Betty struggled violently and wrestled free. She got off the bed, re-arranging her clothes. Johnny was genuinely surprised.

'You wanted it. Don't pretend you didn't. Why've you suddenly changed your mind?'

'Well, we...we don't know each other, do we?'

'Course we do.'

'I mean know each other well. Not really well, we don't.'

'What's that got to do with it? Blimey, I've known some girls for years and never fancied them like I do you. And that's a compliment.'

Betty was flattered. She smiled, came back to sit on the edge of the bed. 'I'm sorry, Johnny. It's...oh, I can't explain.'

Johnny took her hand. 'Look love, it's - hey - you've got the shakes!'

'I have a bit.'

'You weren't kidding, were you? You really are little Miss Innocent.'

'You make it sound terrible.'

'No, it's not. It's sort of - nice. There's too many of the other kind.' Johnny's ardour had subsided. 'Hey, what about that cuppa? It'll be getting cold.'

'Well, I was just pouring if you remember, when you grabbed me.'

'And you fell back on the bed. Very craftily.'

'I didn't! You pushed me.'

'All right. It was all me. I told you I'm a sex maniac, didn't I? I warned you.'

'And I still don't believe you. Sugar?'

'Two please. Ta.'

They sat on the divan again. Betty handed him his tea.

'You're not angry with me?'

'Angry? What's it look like, stupid.'

Betty was on the verge of tears.

'Here, what's the waterworks for?'

'It's just that I feel so horrible. I mean to you. Making you want to, and then...'

Johnny put his tea down. 'Just tell me you wanted to. That's all.' He felt a bit bewildered. What had come over him all of a sudden? Good job some of his mates couldn't see him. That old ram Johnny Dixon playing it all like a favourite uncle to this chick. Something about her waif-like face and unsophisticated charm had caught his heart, made him feel protective for the first time in his life. He kissed her on the mouth, gently.

'No, Johnny, we mustn't start again.'

'So long as I know it wasn't because it was me. Because you didn't want me. It wasn't, was it?'

'If I say that, you'll make me.'

'Make you? Me force you?'

'If you knew I wanted you - yes, you might.'

'All I'm asking you is to say, straight out, that even when you said "no" you really wanted me. No ulterior motives, honest! Now I can't say fairer, can I?'

'You are angry. I can tell you are.'

'Only if you didn't want me. Go on. It's true you did, isn't it?'

Betty nodded.

'Say it. Look at me, Betty darlin'. Say "I wanted you, Johnny!".'

'Johnny - yes, I did want you. I wanted you so bad I don't know how I stopped. Well, now you know.'

'That's all right then. Nothing's going to happen. So you can stop worrying. And take that petrified look off your silly little mug.'

'Oh, Johnny.' Betty clutched him hard and close. He kissed her. Then Betty forced her face away and buried it in his chest. She started sobbing.

'Now what have I done?'

'Nothing. It's me. Everything seemed to be going to well

this morning. You gave us a lift, all the way. Got us fixed up here with your Mum. Then I didn't find a job. Now I'm being nasty to you and you're so nice about it. You won't just walk out, will you? Never come back. I couldn't bear it -'

'Hey, I never said a dicky bird about walking out. Come on. Here.' He took out his handkerchief to wipe her eyes. The packet Christine saw him dig up appeared with it.

'Now look, you're very tired. Travelling all night, no sleep, tramping London all day. No wonder you're so miserable. Everything will work out, you'll see. Here. If you wanta be nice to me, you can do me a favour.'

'Course! Anything.'

Johnny gave her the packet. 'Keep this safe till I see you again. I've promised to take Abby to Manchester, and I don't want to have to hawk it around. I could lose it or get it pinched.'

Betty took the package without question, only too glad to do what he asked. She put it on the high old-fashioned mantelpiece.

Johnny put his arms around her.

'You know, you're just about the sweetest bird I've ever asked a favour of.'

She grinned up at him cheekily.

'Bet you say that to all the girls.'

'I don't. Sweet's the last word for most of 'em.'

'What's different about me, then?'

'Well, just now. You didn't even ask me what's in that packet, did you?'

'Nothing to do with me, is it? I'm just keeping it safe for you.'

'Most girls would have said. "What's so special about this? What's in it?" All that flannel.'

'You'd tell me, if I asked you. Wouldn't you?'

'Course I would.' He pecked her a kiss.

'That's all right then.'

As Christine came in, Betty drew away from Johnny self-consciously, but Christine did not seem to have noticed. She was so elated that she wasn't really there. She was still at the Sybil Waite Studio. She was already a successful model.

'Where've you been, Chris? I was getting worried.'

'Some tea going? That fresh?' Christine tried in vain to seem off-hand.

'Just made. You sound pleased with yourself. Have you got a job?'

Christine helped herself to tea. 'I think so.'

Johnny asked: 'Think so? What's that mean? Have you or haven't you?'

'I won't know until four-thirty.'

Betty was excited. 'Well, don't keep us waiting. Tell us. What sort of job? Where?'

Christine calmly sipped her tea, knowing that the pause was tantalising them. She replaced the cup in the saucer deliberately.

'I've got to ring back. I'd rather not talk about it till I'm certain.'

'Sounds like a right fob-off, that does.' Johnny was sceptical.

'No, it isn't. I had a proper interview.'

'And you think you did all right, Chris?'

'I think so - in fact, I know I did.'

'Well, darlin's, I'm afraid that is going to leave me in suspense, as they say. I must be on my way and I won't be back from the North till late Saturday. But I'm free Sunday. What say we go for a drive? Some smashing countryside I could show you round London. I mean, all three of us.'

Betty jumped at the invitation. 'Lovely, eh, Chris?'

'Better count me out. If I get this job, I'll be working.'

'On a Sunday?' Betty was incredulous.

'All weekend.'

'Never mind then,' said Johnny. 'I'll come around Sunday and if you're out pulling in the lolly, Betty and I'll bobby-off alone, all right?'

Betty secretly hoped that was what would happen. She saw in Johnny's eyes that he hoped so too.

'Bye then, kids. Take care.'

'Bye, Johnny.'

He winked a kiss at Betty and went. She shut the door and turned to Christine. 'What's all the mystery.'

'No mystery.'

'What's the job then. Why do you have to work over the weekend?'

Christine triumphantly produced Sybil Waite's card.

'Modelling, of course. What else would I do?'

'Modelling! You don't mean it? You're not kidding me?'

Betty almost jumped up and down in her excitement. It was a genuine pleasure to see her sister's achievement, which Christine acknowledged with a smile.

'I had a fab piece of luck. I was actually being interviewed by Sybil Waite herself when this call came through. Some important rush job. And they need a model. Well, the good ones are all booked up weeks ahead -'

'Are they?'

'Of course! The top ones. Miss Waite said so.'

'Top ones? They want a really top one? And you think you've got a chance?'

'They're looking now, but if no one's able to do it,' Christine took up a modelling pose, 'It's me! Christina Lane!'

'Christina? Get you!'

The girls hugged each other in delight.

Then Betty turned serious. 'You didn't get this one off those notice-boards? It's not for sexy pictures?'

'Now what do you think I am? For heaven's sake, Betty, give me credit for a bit of sense.'

'Sounds funny to me. Working over the weekend. What d'you know about' - she read the card - "The Sybil Waite Studio?" Could be a load of dirty old men using a woman's name to catch girls.'

'Oh, grow up! Sybil Waite's one of the most famous studios in the world. Ask anyone. I met her. In person. She's super. They're spending a lot of money on this job. Taking a place in the country for the weekend. Specially for it.'

'Wish you'd asked Johnny first. He'd know if it's all right.'

Christine picked up her fashion magazine. She thrust it at Betty as she said: 'You do what you like. But I'm not running my life according to the Gospel of St Johnny.'

'This her? On the front?'

'Cover girl. That's how famous she is. And look inside.'

Betty's eyes grew large as she saw the middle-page spread. She looked from the name in the magazine to the name on the card. 'It's the same, same spelling. Exact.'

'Of course it is.' Christine spotted the packet on the mantel-piece.

'What's that?'

'It's something of Johnny's.'

Christine frowned. She immediately identified it as the packet she saw Johnny collect in the clearing. But before she could pick it up, Betty moved in front of her and took it herself.

'He's asked me to keep it safe for him.'

'Why?'

'I dunno. Just till he gets back from Manchester, that's all. I don't want to pry into his affairs. Don't look so suspicious. It can't be a bomb, that size, can it?' Betty put the packet in her handbag and snapped the clasp in a gesture of finality.

Christine realised that she still hadn't told Betty about Johnny's escapade on the journey. And somehow it still wasn't the right time. She was too full of her own fortunes. The packet could wait until later. Betty was leaping through the magazine again.

'Are you satisfied now? Or do you still think I'm going to be kidnapped by white slave traders or something?'

'Well, you are going off with perfect strangers. Anything could happen.'

'You're beginning to sound like Dad.'

'Don't!' They both laughed - the tension eased.

'Why don't you come along too if you're worried?' asked Christine.

'Would that be allowed?'

'I'll say you're my chaperone. Why not?'

'But what about Johnny? On Sunday?'

'He was talking about driving you somewhere in the country. Tell him to come and collect you. If he's that keen, he will.'

Betty was still doubtful. 'I suppose so. Anyway, we don't know you've got the job yet.'

Christine smiled a secret smile. 'I think you'll find I have.'

And she was right. She had got the job. Betty sat in the back of Sybil's Citroen Safari and pondered over her sister's uncanny sixth sense. Christine had been like this even when they were quite small - suddenly knowing what to do and when to do it - able to predict coming events to an extent that startled her family and, even more, the neighbours. 'That odd child at Number Sixteen' she'd heard them say many times. The thing was that Chris was always right. So Betty followed her unquestioningly. For one thing, it was easier not to have to make the decisions and for another, she loved her sister and admired her, wholly without envy. Now once again she found herself trailing happily in Christine's wake as the car purred smoothly through the attractive Surrey countryside.

Betty had felt a bit overawed by Sybil Waite when she drove up to collect them from the digs early in the morning. She was so very smart and self-possessed, although not the least bit snobby or unkind. After the introductions she had virtually ignored Betty and focused all her attention on Christine, sitting beside her in the front. But Betty had been suddenly conscious that her favourite dress looked cheap and fussy beside Sybil's simple line two-piece. Heaven knows how hard she'd saved to buy it! She had a quick stab of worry about the other clothes she had packed for the weekend. Would they all be out of place? Her glance strayed to the cheap expanding suitcase the two girls were sharing for the trip. It looked rather pathetic on the back seat besides Sybil's crocodile dressing case and matching beauty box. Betty suppressed a sigh. She'd always longed for a really luxurious set of matching luggage, like you saw with film stars. Perhaps one day - when she got married.

Christine didn't feel the same awkwardness. She was quite at ease, leaning forward eagerly in her seat, looking around and taking everything in. She and Sybil had been chatting away during the journey - mostly 'shop talk'. Betty found it all fascinating and Christine was avid for every scrap of information she could pick up. She didn't intend to make any mistakes if she could help it.

'Peter Martin is my photographer,' Sybil was telling her. 'You'll find him very easy to work with. He's a bright lad, going to make a name for himself.'

'I've heard of him,' Christine replied - and then in a confident tone which belied the words: 'I hope he likes me.'

Sybil permitted herself a chuckle. 'Very little doubt about that. He's the first to appreciate a good model. You could have a bright future, Christina. Providing you keep your head.'

'Oh, I will!'

'I've heard so many girls say that, I've lost count. They

throw their careers straight down the drain. A little success, and it goes straight to their heads - they think they know it all. They get so you can't tell them anything. They go overboard completely, whether it's a man, or a boy, or several men. And unless they put first things first that's the end of a promising and very lucrative career.'

'I'm not like that. I know what's important to me, Miss Waite.'

'Sybil. We don't use surnames in this business.'

Christine was revelling in every minute of the journey. Fancy doing this and getting paid for it! Although, she reflected Sybil hadn't talked about money at all. Anyway, it was bound to be more than she'd ever earned before.

Betty still hadn't heard anything she could fault. Yet the more she listened, the less she liked the whole business. Something isn't quite...She couldn't even find the word. She sat silently throughout the drive, trying to decide what it was. And she was no nearer when Sybil just cleared the gateposts as she drove into Wychwold.

It was a near thing. Sybil was taking one hand off the wheel to point to a group of Druid Stones on a wooded hill. 'Look up there! That's the old Witches' Ring.'

The girls looked where she was pointing. Christine was already full of suppressed excitement about the job - now she saw the setting she was to work in, she almost choked. The feeling welled up inside her like a physical pain. She couldn't speak. Her eyes grew large and mystical, her fingers played about her mouth, her gaze darted from place to place, making sure she did not miss anything. Sybil glanced at her. A sardonic and satisfied smile did nothing to enhance her mouth.

'Some parts of Wychwold are quite historic.' The car rounded the final bend in the drive and the house was straight ahead. 'Well, we made it in one piece. We're here.'

Now it was Betty's turn to react. She looked at the house as it came into view: a large, mock-Tudor structure, fairly typical of the richer parts of the Home Counties. To Betty it seemed very grand, yet, in some undeniable way, slightly sinister. The front of the house was in shade, making the dark brick seem almost black. The grounds stretched away as far as she could see. Beautiful lawns, brilliant flower beds, woods in the distance. As they swept round a large circular flower bed to the front door, she got a glimpse of the magnificent terraces at the back. She caught her breath.

'What a heavenly place!' she exclaimed, immediately aware of the inadequacy of the statement.

Sybil smiled agreement. 'It does rather take one's breath away at first sight, doesn't it?'

Christine's mind was on the job. 'It's a super background for fashion pictures.'

As they left the car and crunched across the pink gravel, Sybil felt she should begin preparing Christine a little - not too much, just: 'Er...We won't be using the house all that much. The shots I'm after are more...natural. The river and the woods, nature in the raw, as they say. There are some lovely backgrounds to work against on the estate...'

'You use this place a lot then?'

'Whenever I can. You're not the only girl to do her fist professional job here.'

Christine thrilled to hear herself called 'professional' even obliquely.

Before they reached the door, shouts of 'Sybil, darling!' from the grounds, heralded the breathless arrival of a young man in trendy casual clothes, running towards them. He went straight into Sybil's arms and kissed her profusely if somewhat dispassionately.

'Sybil! Darling ! Good trip down? Much traffic?'

'Very smooth, wasn't it, girls? Christina, this is Peter Martin.'

Peter took Christine's hand warmly. He could hardly get out his 'Hi, Christina,' before adding: 'You didn't exaggerate a bit, Sybil. Not one bit. She's absolutely gorgeous!'

Christine had never before heard anyone compliment her so openly about her looks. She didn't know whether to say 'Thank you', or accept it as if it happened all the time. She settled for a modest smile.

'And this is Betty, her twin sister.'

'Hi, Betty.' Peter shook Betty's hand but was still appraising Christine.

Betty was also distracted. 'Oooh look! You lovely creature!'

A beautifully-groomed cat, that had come out to greet Sybil, was rubbing against Betty's legs. She stooped to stroke its jet-black fur and felt relaxed for the fist time since they left town.

Sybil explained: 'That's Lucifer. He seems to like you. He doesn't usually allow strangers to stroke him. Thank you, Wendell, all the cases please.'

'Certainly Miss Waite.'

The two girls stared at the solemn faced butler who was extracting the baggage from the car. Then they exchanged amused glances. Who'd have thought - even just a few days ago - that they'd find themselves weekending in luxury like this. A place that boasts a butler of all things!

Peter took Christine's arm as if they were close friends, and walked her towards the house. Clearly he had taken her over as his property from then on. But he talked to Sybil.

'How soon can we make a start? There's a helluva lot to do.'

'Soon as you're set up, darling. You look after your equipment. I'll see Christina is ready when you are.'

Sybil pointed back and down towards the house from the hill which they had just climbed. Their view from the Witches' Ring was framed through an arch made by a stone slab resting across two massive uprights. It reminded Christine a bit of Stonehenge. Not that she'd ever been there, but she'd seen pictures of it at school.

Wychwold seemed surrounded by old English trees from up here. The roof and swimming pool were about all that could be seen. The terrace and gardens were hidden, drowned in a sea of summer leaves.

Christine was standing in the centre of the circle of stones, trying to soak in the atmosphere. 'It's a funny name - Wychwold. Does it mean anything? I've got a feeling it does, somehow.'

'Wold means piece of open land or moor; any lonely spot, really. So it's a witches' meeting place. A tryst. The village of Wychwold has a long history of witchcraft.'

'It's fascinating! The whole place. Each time you tell me something about it, I want to know more.'

'You must have a long talk with Gerald, then. My friend

who owns the house. He's the best authority on the subject.'

Sybil saw that Christine's eyes were glowing as she walked round the circle, her hand touching the rough-hewn surfaces of the stones, as if she was compelled to make contact with them.

'You can feel it, can't you? A sort of...atmosphere.'

'I've never brought anyone up here before who's taken to the place like you, Christina.'

'I can't explain it, I just...just like it here. I feel...sort of...at home. As if I'd been here before.'

Sybil was watching her reactions intently. 'The witches used to dance here at dawn. Some people say they still do.'

'Why not? If they did years ago, why not now?'

'Why not indeed. Now, let me show you the river. It flows through the grounds. This way down.'

They grasped hands to prevent each other running too fast down the steep winding path. Their grip was tight, hand fitting hand to perfection.

And as they walked along the river bank, its rippling watery sounds backing their conversation, they still held hands, neither thinking to break the link.

'I was telling you about girls losing their heads. My worst risk is the one-man girl. Girls who are man mad, you know, after anything in trousers, they can get by and still do the job. It's when a model goes overboard for the one-and-only-in-the-world and she listens to him instead of me. That's the trouble. You'd think they'd have some loyalty, after all I've done for them. But they don't, you know. I suppose it's a symptom of the age - no sense of permanence.'

'They want their heads seen to.' Christine really meant it.

'You have the right approach, Christina. But I must repeat I've heard girls swear blind, it's the career and nothing else. Then...there's this one young man and wham! It's all over. They're ringing up the nappy service before you can say Wedding Bells.'

'I'm a career girl! I'll swear on the Bible if you like - but you can probably tell.'

'Boyfriends don't interest you at all?'

'Not seriously. I can take them or leave them alone. I'm not crazy about trousers - except when I wear them myself.'

Christine nearly tripped over a root, washed out of the bank by years of flowing water. Sybil caught her, and held her for a brief moment longer than was necessary. Christine regained her footing.

'Thanks!'

'I must say, you don't strike me as the nappy service type.'

Christine bubbled with laughter. 'There's not a man alive could make me settle for that. Not when...there's all this.'

Sybil led her from the river bank and they reached a narrow patch into the gardens. The scent of herbs pervaded the country air like incense. Christine sniffed ecstatically.

'That smell, Sybil! It's gorgeous. What is it?'

'Gerald grows a lot of herbs. Nature-food - that sort of thing. Some of the villagers think he's a bit of a crank.'

Christine inhaled deeply like a chain-smoker.

'That's hemlock you're smelling now. Very heavy, isn't it?'

'It has heavy effects too. Don't witches use hemlock in their brew?'

'You seem to know a lot about it.' Sybil's penetrating gaze searched her face. Did she know more than appeared from her naive provincial personality?

'I've read a bit. I got a book out of the library once. Don't know why it interests me, but it does.'

'The supernatural is fascinating, Christina. The hypnotic of the unknown.'

'Yes.' Christina turned and their eyes met. They stopped in their tracks involuntarily. 'Yes, I think that's it. It sort of...draws me. Yes.'

But the spell was broken as Peter shouted from the terrace.

'Sybil! Do you want these cider pix done today or not?'

They turned to see him running down the stone steps then across the velvet lawn to reach them quickly. 'Have you seen the time? The light goes an hour before sunset, you know. And we've a lot to get through.'

'I'm sorry Peter. I've been showing Christina around and we got carried away. Nip in and change, dear. The jeans and shirt we brought from the studio.'

Christina didn't need to be told twice. She hared off, her long agile stride cutting corners off flower beds and making her breasts bounce with an excitement that matched her exultation.

They watched her go, pleasurably, in the knowledge she was theirs to use. Peter, who might have been expected to comment on the rear view of Christine as she disappeared all too quickly, said in a matter of fact tone: 'I don't know what ideas you've got for selling this cider with a girl's body, but I'll tell you something - it's revolting stuff to drink.'

'Serves you right for trying the samples. No will-power, that's your trouble, Peter.'

'They've sent three dozen bottles of the stuff. One of Nuits St Georges would have been more appreciated.'

'The way we sell the product has nothing to do with its taste. It's strictly an association of ideas. The copy will imply - very subtly - if you drink this brand of cider, your girl looks like this with her clothes off. And she'll positively beg you to seduce her.'

Peter laughed. 'Not a bad free gift scheme.'

'I'm serious. We imply it. The customer gets the message.'

'Almost subliminal.'

'That girl,' Sybil lingered sensuously over the words, 'will sell anything to any normal male.'

Betty was cuddling the black cat lovingly. Lucifer's purring sounded quite loud in the quiet of the bedroom. It was as different a scene from their own room or their bedsitter in London as could be. Everything was of the best, from the flock-patterned wall-paper to the Florentine lamp-standard and the carved mahogany bed-head. She was curled up on the golden-sheened quilt, her bare toes involuntarily stroking its super-smoothness.

Christine bounded in, unzipping the back of her dress before she had the door closed. 'What are you moping up here for? All by yourself.'

'There's nothing for me to do. I'm not wanted for anything. I feel in the way. I'm beginning to wish I hadn't come.'

Christine stepped out of the dress, revealing that she had only white briefs underneath.

'For heaven's sake why? It's a gorgeous place, you said so

yourself.'

'The place, yes. But I can't keep looking at the walls, even if they are covered in fabulous pictures. Sybil's friend must be loaded to afford all this.'

'You talk as though there's something wrong in being rich. Wish I had a home like this. Wouldn't worry me. Relax! Enjoy yourself.'

Christine threw her dress at Betty. 'This the bathroom?'

'Yes. In there.'

'Never had a bedroom with its own bath before. This is living, Betty! At last we're really living.'

Christine swung into the bathroom and stopped dead in her tracks. She gasped with delight. Bare-breasted Christines were reflected in mirrors on all sides. She saw views of herself she'd never seen before; in profile, three-quarters frontal, even her back view looked super. She looked this way and that way, saw her hair swinging late after her head. She swung it hard, exulting in the effect it created. Suddenly, Betty was behind her at the door.

'What's all that about? What are you doing?'

Christine threw her head back, stretched her arms down to her sides and raised herself on tiptoe. 'I'm looking at the latest Venus, Christina Lane.'

'You're what? Have you gone mad or something? You're letting this go to your head, Chris. Stop it. Stop posing like that.'

'Stop it? Why? What's wrong with looking at yourself in the mirror? I've seen you do it. How often do we get a chance like this? Take your clothes off. Come on! It's marvellous.'

'I will not.'

'Come on. Quick. We haven't much time. They're waiting for me.'

Christine, as if intoxicated, grabbed at Betty. Betty protested, but Christine just laughed and swung her round to undo her blouse, and then her bra. Betty struggled but it was no use.

'There! Look! Ever seen yourself like that before? Have you ever? Isn't that something!'

Betty looked and started to say: 'You must be going off your -' then began to take in the different views. She had to look. In the double-mirrored reflection her breasts seemed slightly different, nicer she thought. She didn't realise the difference was that normally a mirror image was not a true picture, because it reversed everything. Double-mirrors gave the truthful reflection. Christine was right again! Neither of them had seen herself like that before.

'What wouldn't Johnny give to see you now?'

'Oh, Christine! Please!' cried Betty as she slipped free and dashed into the bedroom.

It was the first time she'd felt embarrassed with Christine before. Her cheeks were tingling as she touched them with the palms of her hands.

Christine laughed as she caught several mirrored versions of herself again and suddenly disliked her white briefs. She closed the bathroom door quietly. Then slowly began to reveal a multi-picture of complete nakedness. She was excited by what she saw. She'd known she had a good figure, but framed in this luxury setting, an almost 3D effect, all these angles of her... What a fool she was to jib at showing herself to Sybil at the studio. No wonder she'd asked her to do nudes. Christine had forgotten that was before she took her clothes off.

Her reverie was disturbed by a distant shout from Peter on the terrace.

'Chris! Come on!' She dashed out into the bedroom.

'Those jeans! That shirt! Where are they, Betty?'

Betty was stretched out full-length on the golden quilt.

'Where you left them. Still in the case.'

Christine grabbed the jeans and pulled them up over her slender limbs.

Betty watched her as she zipped them up.

'Those are a man's! Chris - you've got nothing on underneath!'

'Don't want any lines showing through these tights pants. It'd spoil the picture.'

Christine clipped the waistband and grabbed the shirt. Betty got up off the bed.

'And the shirt. That's a man's too.'

'I know. That's the idea. Sybil says it gives the right image to the product. The girl is in a wood, dressed in her boyfriend's clothes.'

'What's she getting at?'

'That he's taken her clothes off and she's taken his, I suppose. These are his shirt and pants. It's sexy!'

'Chris! What's come over you?'

'Nothing. We're not in the provinces now. You've got to catch on to these things pretty quick.'

'I don't see how that makes an advert. What are you supposed to be selling?'

'Cider. You going to have another look? In there?' Christine pointed at the bathroom door as Betty, still bare-breasted, approached it.

'Cider?'

'You'll see what sells. In those mirrors.'

Betty turned at the door. 'I'm going to pick up my blouse and bra. It'll give me something to do - mending the damage you've done.'

Christine smiled her winning smile. Betty smiled back.

'You do have some funny ideas, Chris. I don't know where you get them from. Honestly!'

'Nor do I,' laughed Christine. 'It's just the way I'm made, I guess.'

Peter was getting impatient. He shifted his camera strap to the other shoulder.

'What's she doing, having a bath?'

Sybil was beginning to think this girl was going wrong in the fastest time ever. After all she said, too! Typical!

'Go and find her. If she is, burst in and drag her out.'

But before Peter could take one step, Christine came running towards them so fast it made Sybil feel out of breath to watch her. She looked wonderful. The shirt and jeans were a great idea.

'Sorry. My sister -'

Sybil cut her off. She was firm but not sharp.

'There's no excuse for unpunctuality in this business, Christina. Either you're dead on time or you've missed the session. Whatever the reason, it's your job to be there. Ready to work. No excuses are good enough. That's all there is to it. Right. Now Peter, that little glade in the woods I mentioned...'

'Let's go then. While the sun's just right, filtering through the branches. Super if we can catch it before it sinks any lower.'

'Off you go then.' Sybil demonstrated her complete confidence in Peter by walking back towards the house without giving any more instructions.

Peter led the way along the herb-scented path to the copse which marked the perimeter to the formal gardens. Christine suddenly called to mind that once she went into a wood with a boy at home. Henry, a machine-minder in the car factory down the road. She'd had to run for her life. All Henry had tried to do was put his hand on her blouse. On the outside! Funny to think of it now! How innocent can you be?

'What are you laughing at?' Peter asked as they reached the trees and left the high summer light behind.

'Was I?'

'I don't mind. But keep that expression when we start shooting, for the first few shots anyway.' He was anxious to get going. Christine looked very lovely. Sunbeams flickering through the tree-tops highlighted the sheen on her long hair.

Peter unclipped his camera. He looked round. One tree seemed the same as another to Christine, but clearly there was a difference photo-wise. He began to grumble that he couldn't find exactly what he was looking for. At last: 'This one! Perfect! Come here, darling.'

He took hold of her arms and leaned her back against a sloping tree trunk, just like an interior decorator draping a gathered curtain artistically.

Peter stood back, checking through his viewfinder.

'No, not quite what I want.' He went back to her and put his hands under her arms. He lifted her gently, then turned her slightly. Thinking she was being helpful, she twisted her body with him.

'No, darling, leave it to me. When you've more experience, you'll be told what to do. But not yet. Not for some time yet.' He turned her back so slightly it was hardly noticeable.

'Look, love, relax. Completely relax. Put yourself in my hands.' He moved her left arm by a slight pressure on her elbow. Christine let it happen. She surprised herself how easy it was to let him mould her into the shape he wanted.

'That's better. Just a prick of sunlight between the arm and body - and hold it! Hold it, darling. Don't move once I've set you up. Not a fraction of an inch. Now you're stiffening again. Oh, for God's sake!'

Peter dashed back to her, scolding. But by the time he reached her his anger had subsided.

'I said don't do anything - except relax. Leave it to me. If I tread on you toe you don't move, never mind scream. Get it? Right.'

His hands seemed to be all over her, adjusting a wisp of hair, tucking her shirt into her jeans, then muttering 'Try it the other way then' to himself and pulling it out all round.

He stood back. Checked again. Christine wondered if he had any feelings for her as a real live girl. Was this really all part of his job? Or was he putting on a big act that he could take this sort of liberty?

She was about to protest when he said: 'Look unzip your jeans and zip them up again to take that crease out. Must be your panties. Are they frillies or something?'

Christine did not reply. Amongst these lonely trees it seemed he could get away with anything. She wished Sybil were there, or even Betty. She really would have liked a chaperone. Or would she? Wasn't this the excitement she'd been looking for? Wasn't it part of the fun of the job? She found herself getting hold of the zip tog and saying: 'I'm surprised you don't do this for me. You weren't so bashful before!'

'I will if you like. I thought you might not have anything on underneath. Doesn't look like it now I look closely.' And he became engrossed in his cameras.

Christine zipped down the jeans with caution. Very carefully she did it up again. It seemed that the photographer was not so absorbed by his lenses as he made out, for at once he was back beside her, posing her against the tree for the second time.

'We've got to work pretty fast before we lose that shaft of light across your legs.' She felt this must be the final appraisal before he started taking pictures, but no. 'Er...Okay, I think. Except...' He's back again. 'We need just a fraction of bosom showing. To attract the randy customers.'

He was already placing Christine's arms back from her shoulders around the tree-trunk. After his earlier remonstrations she held them as if they were tied there, even though his slender fingers were busy undoing the buttons of her shirt. She'd left two unfastened herself. Peter worked down until only the very bottom one was doing its job. Christine felt that she couldn't even breath deeply. But Peter was already composing his shot and clearly this was what he wanted. She felt provocative. It was a marvellous feeling, the same surge of excitement that came over her in the multi-mirrored bathroom.

But it was still not quite right. Peter lowered his camera and dashed back to her.

'They're too good to waste, darling. I want as much as you've got.' And with two fingers and his thumb, he twitched the last button and the shirt fell apart, revealing Christine's full, firm breasts. She felt the tingle of cool air against them.

Peter's only reaction was 'Whoops, sorry' and he carefully draped the front edges of her shirt so that her lovely breasts showed almost imperceptibly.

'Can't have the boys completely distracted from the product. That's what I want. Great!' Peter had been more appreciative of her attractions than she'd thought. 'Haven't seen anything like these for months. Months! He called as he returned to apply equally precise attention to his camera work.

'Right. Now still, but relaxed. Lovely.' At long last Christine heard the click of his camera shutter. Her very first shot as a professional model. But now he shot. And shot. And shot. Between each exposure he said 'Lovely!' or 'Gooooood!' or 'Keep it like that!' Or 'Great!' or 'Just once more'. And he showed no sign of taking a respite. He knelt below her, ran round the far side of the tree and shot across her, came close and shot down on her. As he reloaded one camera, then the other, she wondered if it cost a fortune in film. Very little in proportion, if she did but know.

'Right! A few action shots now. Try running towards me - leaping, carefree stuff. You know, wild abandon. Just let it go. Get the idea?'

'Yes. I get the idea.' Christine's voice had a query in it.

'But what, love?'

'Well, I can't keep my shirt like this, can I?'

'Course you can't. Oh come on, we're not going all shy are

we? You're being paid for this. Let's have some action.'

Christine heard herself denying her modesty.

'I don't mean that. I thought you didn't want to go any further than this. What did you call it? Distracting the customer from the product?'

'You leave that to me. I'll scrap any shots that go too far. But let's get everything we can on the negative. Out of a dozen or so one or two won't show any erotica. So to speak. There isn't time to explain my job. You do yours right. Now let's have everything you've got. Joie de vivre, bouncy, bouncy, swinging! Ready?' He aimed the camera. 'Go.'

Christine ran at him, leaping and throwing her arms out. She was releasing her energies after being still so long. She knew she looked good. She liked the attention focused on her. She was intoxicated by the camera lens, flattered by its following her round and clicking greedily, asking for more and more visual delight.

Peter kept it going - colour, then black and white, full-lengths, close-ups, faces, legs, breast from all angles. Even through his viewfinder the small image of Christine excited him. Her whole body had natural grace, accentuated by her flowing hair and seductive breasts.

Peter kept her working. Would she be exhausted first? Or his stock of film?

Betty was as indolent as Christine was active. With the black cat sleeping in her lap, she lay in a luxurious cane garden-chair, its flowered pattern competing with the profusion of border flowers that edged the close-cropped lawns. Her eyes were closed in protection against the glorious sun, unobscured here by trees. That cat had curled round to make a nest in her lap and in doing so had pulled up her skirt to flaunt more thigh than Betty realised.

The silence was suddenly oppressive, sinister. She got a feeling she was being watched. She half opened her eyes, without moving. The voyeur was the milkman, a brawny tough-looking chap only a year or two older than herself. He stared lecherously at the tops of her legs, revealed by her drawn up skirt.

Betty clutched the cat, which jumped down as it was rudely awakened. Pretending she had not seen the spectator, she got up and walked quickly towards the house, gradually quickening her pace. The milkman stared after her, enjoying the swing of her skirt against the back of her legs. His mouth dried. No birds in Wychwold were stacked like this chick.

As Betty opened the door to go in, the cat wriggled and ran ahead of her. She turned to close the door and saw Sybil approach the milkman. He pointed at the garden chair. Were they discussing her, she wondered? If so, why?

She closed the door; still wondering. But her thoughts were disturbed by the cat's mewing. At first she couldn't tell where it was coming from. Then she discovered a door built into the panels at the side of the staircase. And it was slightly open. From the direction of the sound, the cat was caught inside there, somehow.

She found the panelled door opened directly onto stone steps, which led down towards what looked like a wine cellar. Racks of bottles, some of them cobwebbed, lined the stone walls. She took a few steps down, following the cat's continued mewing. Lucifer was asking to be allowed through a heavy wooden door at the bottom of the stairs. Perhaps that was where he lived. She carried on down to let him in.

She flicked on an old metal-domed light-switch. The gloom

was reflected by a low-watt bulb suspended on its own flex, now black with age and cobwebs. She pulled at the iron bolt fastening the door and to her surprise it slid back easily. The latch seemed rusty and possibly hard to lift. But it turned out to be well lubricated and worked as smoothly as a door-knob.

She pushed the door open and the cat disappeared silently into the cavernous interior. The naked light-bulb highlighted the square stones which made up the cellar walls. Betty reached in to pull the door when she saw a sight that made her gasp.

She paused, her hand on the latch. The cellar had been transformed into some sort of chapel. She could just make out an altar at the far end. She switched on the cellar light to make sure her eyes didn't deceive her. One end of the windowless room was a raised wooden dais covered with black carpet in contrast to the overall flagged floor.

There was the altar draped in purple velvet. Gleaming brass candlesticks held large black candles. She noticed there was no crucifix, no Bible, no hymn number-board and presumed it was a private chapel, not then in use. She noticed the side walls were decorated with old swords, chains and wrought iron pieces which she could not identify.

But there was something else on the altar. She moved forward to look. There were two objects which seemed quite alien to a chapel - a dagger, set with vivid jewels, and a wicked-looking scouge. Only then did it occur to her that maybe she ought not to be there. She wondered why the cat had asked to be let in and now was nowhere to be seen.

Suddenly the ceiling reverberated as the front door closed overhead. It vibrated through the chapel and was followed by a rustle which made her look up. Bats, hanging from the cross-beams, were swinging upside down. She stifled a feeling of panic and wanted to scream. Then she realised they were dead, stuffed, and only swaying due to the vibrations from the floor above. She ran out, up the stone steps and into the hall.

Sybil was half-way up the main staircase when she heard the panelled door close. She turned to find Betty ashen-faced and trembling on the threshold.

'Are you all right, Betty? You look as if you've seen a ghost.'

'Do I? No...It's...' She felt compelled somehow not to explain, she didn't know why. 'I feel a bit sick. And I've got a headache. So I came down for a breath of air. The cat wanted to go down the cellar so I opened this door for it. Is that all right?'

'Which door?'

'This one. It leads down to the cellar, doesn't it?' she asked innocently.

'Oh yes. Lucifer is allowed the run of the house. Sorry about your head. Wychwold air will soon blow it away.'

'Thank you. I hope so.' Betty went out of the front door.

Sybil stared after her thoughtfully, before continuing up the curve of the wide staircase.

Peter looked at Christine through his viewfinder. Now her shirt was partly buttoned again and she stood on a flat stone, lapped by the river, pushing her big toe into the flowing water. 'Like that! Hold it - right there.'

The shutter clicked. 'You're doing fine. Catching on fast. Now look at the sky. That's it. Perfect. Push them out through the shirt. Make 'em punch two holes in it. Bet you can't.'

Christine smiled at the thought and had a good attempt.

Click. 'Super.' Click. 'Gorgeous.' Click. 'Right. One more angle. Er...let's have the jeans off.'

Christine did no more than raise an eyebrow which he ignored. She looked at him once again. He wasn't joking. He meant it.

'Right off, Peter?'

'Well, not half, dear, what would that be like?'

'You think any man will look at the product?'

'Never mind the product. Come on, before the light starts to go. Maybe we'll get some shots for something else. Drop them, love, come on!'

Christine noticed that Peter wasn't interesting himself in his camera now. He was waiting for the show. All right, she'd give him one.

'You were right, you know. I haven't anything underneath.'

'Not to worry. The shirt's long enough. Just about.'

'I'm not so sure.'

'Well, drop them and we'll find out.'

Christine kept her eyes on his, which were glued to the jeans. She unhooked the waistband slowly, ensuring that as she undid the zip the shirt hung closed and as low as possible. She didn't bend down either, but let the trousers drop down her thighs and shins, keeping her legs fairly close so that they dropped with a slow-motion effect.

Peter took it all in brazenly. Or was it professionally? She couldn't really tell.

He picked up the camera to put it to his eye. But didn't. His voice was a little hoarse.

'You really do have it all, don't you. Those legs, that skin, that hair, those eyes. It's the lot, darling. You've got the bloody lot!'

Christine thrilled inside, but was determined not to show how much she liked his admiration.

'Well, thank me for the compliment.'

'I wasn't sure if you really meant it or were just being professional.'

Peter lowered his camera to hand on its strap. He walked towards the bank and took one stride onto the flat stone. Christine couldn't back away without stepping into the water. She looked at him through half-shut lashes, tempting him, daring him to kiss her.

'Christine, you make it very difficult to concentrate. You know that?'

'Do I?'

'You know damn well you do.'

'I'm only standing here doing exactly what you tell me to do. What do you want next?'

Peter broke one of his cardinal rules. If you want to kiss a model, wait until after the session. Business before pleasure. But his arms went round Christine and their lips came together. It was an idyllic gentle kiss and when Peter drew away first, it was obviously with some effort. Christine hadn't moved at all.

'Do you kiss all your models when you have them half stripped?'

'Never. During working hours.'

'Expect me to believe that?'

'It's true. Rule Number One in the Peter Martin code book.

Honestly.'

'I'm the exception that makes the rule?'

'Shows there's something special about you.'

'Is it part of a model's contract to respond to your advances?'

Peter's hand dropped down her back below her shirt and rested on her bottom. Then he smacked it playfully.

'Behave yourself. Right, back to work. See where the sun is already.'

Peter strode to the bank. 'Right, look back over your right shoulder.' Click. 'Let your hair fall down.' Click.

Christine hoped he was telling the truth. That he didn't usually kiss models while they were working. He seemed genuine. He was obviously attracted by her and this pleased her, gave her a first taste of the power she could have over men. Men who were going to matter - as distinct from boys she'd known who didn't.

'Chris, for a first session you've been great. Slip your jeans on and we'll wrap it up.'

Christine timed the moment he put the lens hoods on his cameras, to pull on her jeans.

'Tell you what, darling? Why don't we walk back the river way? It's nearly as quick. And much more pleasant.'

'Whatever you say.' She looked at him, eyes twinkling with amusement - at once demure and yet provocative. 'You're the boss - here, anyway.'

As Betty strolled across the lawn towards the house, she seemed to have recovered from her visit to the cellar. To see the colour in her cheeks, no one would have guessed anything had happened.

Her path through borders of shrubs bursting with exotic flowers made it hard to believe that under this house there was a weird chapel which must once have been used for some strange ceremonies. Her thoughts were interrupted by the sudden appearance of a man striding towards the front door. He walked smartly, as if dressed in military uniform, although in fact he was wearing expensive country tweeds. He carried a shotgun under his arm. And he was looking at her. He was taking her in, like the milkman had done, if anything more overtly. He did not disguise that he was mentally undressing her.

He smiled, but to Betty it was a leer. He nodded his head courteously and said 'Good-day', and made it sound like 'Come to my place and see my etchings'.

She was both embarrassed and a little apprehensive. Her spine tingled. She was used to boys of her own age looking at her, but this was something quite different. She tried to smile, say 'Good-day' in return, anything to break the fierce inspection, but her lips were tight and unsmiling. She began to tremble with inexplicable fear.

The man seemed surprised that she did not return his greeting. He hitched his gun under his arm and raised his hat, very country-gentleman style. But Betty had the feeling that at any moment he was going to make a grab for her, and madly rip her clothes off. Yet she knew this was all in her mind.

At last Betty found the will to do something and the fact that it must have looked off to the man didn't make any difference. She suddenly ran across the drive, past the main entrance to the house, round the side and on to the terrace. Anything to escape those lecherous eyes, no matter what he thought of her behaviour.

She glanced back over her shoulder to make sure he wasn't following her, and bumped into Sybil Waite who was turning the corner towards her.

'Oh! Miss Waite. I'm sorry. I didn't know anyone was...'

'Betty! Whatever is the matter?'

'Nothing. Nothing really. I...er...'

'Something is. You're trembling, girl. What's wrong? You aren't ill, are you? You're sure it's just a headache?'

'Er...yes. Yes. I just thought - had a thought, I mean. I should have made a phone call but I forgot the time. It's so lovely here. May I use the telephone?'

'Of course. There's one in the library.'

Betty was glad to escape scrutiny. She knew she was not making much sense. And Sybil's eyes were searching hers fiercely.

But it was nothing to what she'd have felt if she could have seen the look Sybil gave her as she ran towards the terrace steps.

It was a look of intense evil, as if she was willing something to happen. Was it coincidence that Betty suddenly missed her footing and sprawled up the terrace steps? As she fell, her head met the stone with some impact and she lay in a heap, very still, across the steps.

Sybil smiled as she moved towards the unconscious girl.

Christine and Peter, hands clasped and arms swinging, were enjoying the river bank walk.

'Dad was so impossible, Peter. We had to get out. There and then. I couldn't have stuck it a minute longer. Perhaps Betty might have, but he'd have taken it out on her. Just as well I talked her into coming with me.'

'And you're not sorry now?'

'What do you think?' Christine kicked at a tuft of grass, pointing her toe subconsciously with the grace of a ballet-dancer.

Suddenly the dull thudding of horses hooves disturbed the silence and a woman galloped at high speed towards them from behind a copse. She was startled by their presence on this little-used path and she only just succeeded in pulling up. The horse reared, towering over Christine and Peter. Christine screamed. Peter side-stepped to the flank of the horse's exposed belly and grabbed the reins, almost swinging on them.

'Let go! What are you doing? I can control her.'

The woman half-threatened to crack her riding crop across Peter's hands. But he hung on and pulled the horse down, soothing it as he did so.

'Steady there. Steady.' His voice was cool. He patted its head, tickled behind its ear.

Christine had backed a safe distance away. The bank was narrow at this point, certainly not wide enough to gallop past two people side by side. Peter was angry.

'That's a damn silly thing to do. Coming round the bend at that pace!'

The woman, elegant in full riding gear, smiled. It was clear she thought he'd panicked over nothing. She touched her peaked cap with her crop in a mock salute and rode on. The horse almost knocked Christine into the water as it broke into a canter.

'You all right, Christine?'

'Just about. Scared me a bit.'

'She's got a nerve. She really has!'

'Who is she?'

'Oh, she lives round here.'

'You know her?'

'No, not really.'

'She seems to know you.'

'I've seen her in the village. Come on, I've got an idea for one more series of shots. You game?'

'Of course. What is it?'

'Using the old boathouse as a background. It isn't far now.'

The horsewoman had galloped away from the bank and into a spinney. She pulled up and swung the animal's head round sharply. She stood in the stirrups and stared back towards Peter and Christine as they reached the copse on the bend of the river.

Christine felt compelled to look round. She couldn't see the horsewoman staring after her. But she felt somehow that she was.

'Peter.'

'Yes?'

'Do you get the feeling we're being watched?'

'Here? Apart from the galloping madwoman, now over the hill and far away, I don't suppose there's another living person for a couple of miles. This is private land belonging to the house. She has Gerald's permission to ride over it, unfortunately.'

'I'll be glad when we get to the boathouse.'

Peter stared at her, remembering what she had looked like earlier. 'So will I,' he laughed.

Betty was lying on her bed again. But this time, although Lucifer nestled beside her, she was unaware he was there. She was very still, eyes closed, face and toes upturned towards the ceiling, her arms by her sides.

Her lids flickered and her eyes opened. Her face showed she was confused, wondering where she was. She tried, with an effort, to sit up. But a hand gently but firmly dissuaded her.

She turned her eyes to identify the owner. He was a stranger, handsome with greying hair and attractive, if piercing eyes. He was elegantly, yet far from formally dressed. He stood close to the side of the bed, his hand holding her shoulder down so that her head remained on the pillow. His smile was reassuring.

For a moment, Betty wondered if she was actually in bed. She managed to look down at herself and found that she was dressed and lying on the quilt. Then she began to wonder what had happened, the last she remembered was...

'Don't worry, don't worry. You're all right, my dear. It was a nasty fall. You knocked your head on the stone steps and I'm afraid good Carrara marble is pretty hard as well as beautiful. It's been here much longer than we have.' He touched her temple lightly and she felt the tender pain of a bruise.

'Just lie still for a while. That's the only treatment you need. Here, come along, Lucifer, don't disturb the little lady.' He picked up the cat and planted it in his own lap. He sat beside the bed as if intending to stay with her indefinitely.

Betty was still frightened. So far as she could see there was on one else in the room. Who was this man?

'Yes, but -' she began.

'No "buts" about it. You're suffering from shock. Just a little. Rest is the only answer. Shakes you up, something like that.' Then, as if reading her thoughts, he added: 'Oh I should have introduced myself. My name is Amberley. Doctor Gerald Amberley. This is my house.'

Betty smiled with relief, from her own foolish imagination.

He stroked the cat's fur, seeming to get as much pleasure from it as the cat did. 'I'm sorry I wasn't here when you arrived. But I see Lucifer took to you immediately. He is rather choosy. But we usually like the same people.'

'He's beautiful. I like him, too.'

'That's splendid. Sybil tells me you seemed to be running away from something? What frightened you? So strange. My garden is designed for tranquillity.'

'It's lovely here. It really is.'

'But something must have scared you?'

Betty was embarrassed. 'It seems so silly now.'

Gerald still stroked Lucifer. 'It must have seemed real enough at the time. Besides, anything that happens under my roof...I feel responsible for.'

'It didn't. Not under your roof, I mean.'

'While you are my guest, I feel responsible. What could possible happen in my garden to frighten you?'

'You'll think I'm stupid, I'm sure you will.'

Gerald shook his head. He removed his hand from the cat and held hers, squeezing it reassuringly.

'Well, first it was the milkman.' Betty blushed furiously. She realised how ridiculous it sounded.

'The milkman. Our milkman?'

'I was sort of dozing and I suddenly realised he was standing on the path, looking at me, staring. In a funny sort of way. It gave me the shivers.'

'How d'you mean, funny?'

'I can't explain exactly. The way he looked just made me feel...sort of frightened.'

'Of our milkman?'

'No, I mean just frightened. So I got up to go back into the house.' And again, for some reason she couldn't admit to herself, she found she purposely avoided mentioning what she saw in the cellar.

Gerald Amberley was much too gallant to be derisive. 'Is that all?'

'Well,...I didn't actually stay in more than a few minutes. I decided to go for a walk, get some fresh air. I had a bit of a headache anyway.'

'And something else happened on this walk?'

'Oh dear! It sounds so stupid when you say it. It was probably all my imagination. Chris, my sister, is always saying I think far too much.'

'That's possible. We all do sometimes. What was it you might have imagined?'

'This man with a gun. Oh, I don't mean I imagined him. But the way he looked at me. So strange, weird almost. And it was like - well, it seemed to me to be like - the look in his eyes was very much like the milkman's.'

'A military-looking gentleman? Moustache?'

'Yes, that's right.'

'Colonel Cruickshank. He told me how you'd reacted. He was rather concerned that you were one of those people who are frightened at the sight of a gun.'

Betty sighed with relief. 'Oh, I am sorry, doctor. Please forgive me. Making all this bother.'

'No bother at all.' He let go of her hand, patted her cheek. 'Tell me, this look they both gave you, can you describe it? I mean was it a look of recognition, or...or what?'

'No, they didn't recognise me. They'd never seen me before.'

'Of...disapproval, then?'

'Oh, no.'

'The opposite. They liked the look of you?'

'Yes, I suppose more that way.'

Gerald smiled. 'You shouldn't mind men admiring you.'

'It was more than that...more...' Betty couldn't think of a way of putting it that wouldn't make her sound conceited.

Gerald Amberley tried for her. 'You think they were looking at you as if to say "I wish she were my girl. I wouldn't mind, er... How shall I put it these modern days?...taking her off for a rave-up weekend!"'

'Well, yes. Except they didn't seem to be thinking about a weekend so much as...' Again she couldn't find the words to use, even to a doctor.

'They were...desiring you? There and then?'

Betty looked down. 'Yes, I suppose that was it... I said it would sound stupid.'

'Not at all. All it proves is that they're both quite normal. There'd be something odd about them if they didn't have their heads turned by a pretty girl like you. You dress attractively. You have...may I be frank?'

Betty looked at him without answering a tacit 'yes'.

'Well now. Quite clinically - let us examine the problem.'

He stood, carefully putting the cat on the floor. Then he bent slightly over the bed, his hands hovering above her face. Betty drew in a breath and held it. She felt terribly vulnerable, exactly the same feeling she tried to describe to this man only a few minutes ago.

'Don't stiffen up, dear. Just lie back and concentrate on what I'm hoping to demonstrate to you.'

Betty tried. And wondered if her skirt was lying flat against her legs. She thought she could feel it but didn't dare look, or even draw attention to her thoughts by moving her hands from her sides to pull at it.

'That's better. Now, we'll start at the top. Your hair-style. You do it this way because it suits you best? For your particular type of looks?'

'Yes. I read in a magazine - about the way to do it for my shape of face.'

'Quite right.' He touched her hair, so light that if she hadn't been watching him she wouldn't have known. 'And lovely hair it is. Now your face. Beautiful skin, not a blemish. Not a wrinkle. You use very little make-up, so you must be aware that your face doesn't need artificial help to improve it.'

'I don't know about that, doctor.' By calling him doctor she was reassuring herself, or trying to. There was an inner battle going on between pleasure at his compliments, which every girl would like to hear, and apprehension at what they might be leading up to.

'Your eyes are bright, a lovely colour and framed in gorgeous lashes. Your lips are what the old type of women's magazines my sisters used to read called "eminently kissable". These are facts, not just my opinion.'

For a moment she thought he was going to bend down to kiss her, but he was only examining her closely, as if it were her tonsils that were under inspection.

'Now, look at your figure. I mean, I'm looking at it. You can't very well - not while you're lying there, can you?' He smiled at his little joke. 'Compare it with most girls or you age. With older girls. And with women's figures. Not the glamorous pictures of film stars and bikini girls. I'm talking about the women we see from day to day, in our ordinary lives. You are in beautiful proportion, nice long neck -' He stroked her neck gently. '- Good shoulders, gently sloping, not bony.' He gripped her shoulders in confirmation and then let go. 'And very nice breasts.' Betty froze. She reminded herself that he was a doctor. If she were ill she might have had to take her clothes off. The thought flashed through her head in the moment of time that his hand hovered, indicating the contours of her bust, and was withdrawn.

Gerald smiled. 'Do you wear a brassiere?' He used the French pronunciation, even to the final 'r'.

'Yes.' She wondered at the question.

'Why?'

'Well...I always have. I mean, ever since I...since I needed to.'

'But why do you need to? Some girls don't these days, do they?'

'No. My sister doesn't sometimes.'

'Have you ever thought why you always do?'

'No. I haven't, I suppose.'

'Then let's take it one stage further. You don't wear just any sort of brassiere, do you? You give some thought to it. The shape, the style, the material it's made of.'

'Oh, yes.'

'What influences your choice?'

'Well, one that suits me.'

'That looks nice?'

'Yes.'

'One that...does something for you?'

'Yes of course. Must do.'

'One that shows off your figure to best advantage. So that your breasts look as attractive as you can possibly make them through your summer dress?'

'Yes, I suppose so. I'd never thought about it as much as that.'

'In fact, to make you very desirable.'

'I wouldn't go that far.'

'But you do go that far, Betty. If you succeed, any normal man is going to find you desirable. Look at the way your dress is shaped tight into that slim waist, how its length is just right to show off your pretty legs. Do you consider you have pretty legs? Has that ever occurred to you?'

'Not really. Chris has the legs in our family.'

'Possibly she had, but that doesn't mean that yours haven't a fascination - a visual fascination - that catches a man's eye too. Slim ankles many a rich woman would give a fortune for.' His fingers and thumb measured her ankles like callipers, then his hand slipped smoothly up her leg in keeping with his comments. 'Nice non-muscular calves, smooth knees. You mean to say you've never noticed that?'

'No. Not really.'

His hand continued to move slowly. But Betty lifted her hands from her sides to join in her lap, causing a depression in the middle of her skirt, and acting as a chastity belt as in medieval days. Gerald smiled and removed his hand from her leg.

'You are too modest, my dear. Take a good look at yourself, sometime. Think how attractive you must seem to all kinds of men. Don't take fright when they look at you -' He gave her a very attractive, non-lecherous smile '- with the lust of life in their eyes.'

'I see what you mean.'

'Either that, or put on a false nose, bind your chest flat and wear the ugliest clothes you can find. Do you fancy that?'

'Heavens no!'

'Well, then! And in any case, men haven't got the monopoly on sexual fantasies. So don't be too hard on them. Plenty of young girls have them - young girls particularly. Especially if they've led repressed lives. You've come to London from the Midlands, Sybil tells me.'

'Yes, we have.'

'Parents very strict?' She nodded. 'Boyfriends all trying to seduce?'

'Dad didn't ever say it as frankly as that, but that's what he was on about all right. He would go mad if he thought I'd been out with a boy, or even a group of us, boys and girls.'

'A classic case. Text book. In spite of the fact that you are so attractive, Betty...And you find men desire you...You are, I'm almost sure of this, but I will ask...You are still a virgin?'

Betty nearly died. What a direct question! She closed her

eyes, swallowed. It was such a personal matter, the most intimate question that she'd ever been asked. Then she remembered again he was a doctor. Oh, if only she were more like Chris! She'd come straight out with the answer, and not feel embarrassed like this.

'You don't have to answer, if you don't wish to. I am certain that you are.'

Her legs began to tremble and feel weak. She was sure he could see the tremor which she felt from her toes right to the very top of her legs. She was grateful when he pretended not to and put one hand on each knee to steady them. Immediately the trembling stopped.

His voice was calm, almost whispering to her. 'It's a phase, Betty. A beautiful phase in your life. A girl of ten yearns to be twelve. You look forward to your twenties. A virgin looks forward to losing her virginity.'

She couldn't quite make out whether his hands were gently pulling at her knees or whether it was her awakening desire for him. And she didn't want that. Oh no! She'd refused Johnny. If it was going to be anybody, it must be Johnny, not this - this man. She told herself yet again he was a doctor. A doctor! But he was a man too. He'd said how attractive she was. That meant he must find her desirable himself - as a man, not as a doctor. She was gasping now, her breasts heaving, stretching the front of her dress until she felt it would burst open.

His voice was still cool, and so quiet she had to concentrate to hear him. His hands were quite still, lightly moving between her knees in a kind of caress. Ignoring them, he said: 'One day - perhaps quite soon - you'll meet a man - a young man, probably, who knows? - and suddenly you'll like the way he looks at you - his desire for you won't panic you at all. You will go to him, all the way - not run away from him. He will take you and you will take him, just as eagerly. It could happen anytime, probably just when you least expect it. You won't be able to do a thing about it. And you won't want to.'

Betty heard her voice almost hoarse: 'You make it sound so...natural.'

'Isn't that exactly what it is? The most natural thing in the world. What is there to fear in nature?'

'I suppose I'll get over this silly attitude. You've helped me, doctor. Really you have.'

Gerald took his hands from her knees as if he had just finished checking for broken bones.

'Promise me you will think of me - of what I've said - when it happens again. Don't worry your pretty head any more.'

'I'll try.'

'Now then.' He moved towards the bathroom. 'I prescribe a hot bath. Luxuriate in it. Nothing like it for calming the nerves.'

He disappeared into the Hall of Mirrors and she heard the water tumbling at force into the bath.

Gerald returned to the bed, holding out a hand for her. She took it and he led her into the bathroom.

'You're looking better already.'

Betty could see herself several times. And Gerald too. He was very handsome for an older man. Older by her own age group, she corrected herself. She would bet he was a heartbreaker to girls in, say, their twenties.

'You'll find plenty of soaps, perfumes, bath-salts. Oh, but you mustn't use those if you don't want to enhance your attractions.' He smiled kindly.

Did he expect her to start undressing while he was still there? Did he think he was going to undress her himself? Oh dear, she'd already forgotten his advice. Surely there was nothing further from his mind. Was there, she wondered?

She decided to find out, to make it pointed enough.

'Thank you doctor. I am feeling much better.' And her hand went to the top button of her dress, indicating that she wished to undress. His eyes focused on her fingers, now very still. He took one step nearer. Then he kissed her in a fatherly fashion on the forehead. His fingers replaced hers on the button and he expertly slipped it undone.

'There. I'm sure you can manage the rest if you stop allowing your imagination to run away with you.'

He went to the mirrored door and turned.

'You are a virgin aren't you Betty? It's nothing to be ashamed of.'

Betty swallowed: 'Yes, I am.'

She thought she saw that 'desire' look, as he called it, in his eyes. He nodded approval, saying: 'I'm glad you are.' And went out.

Betty sighed as she took her dress off. She was about to undo her bra strap when the door opened again.

It was Gerald with the cat in his arms. Without seeming to notice she now wore only pants and bra, he remarked: 'I'll leave Lucifer with you for company.' The cat was on the floor and the door closed again before she could open her mouth to speak.

Betty bolted the door. As she turned with her hands reaching to the centre of her bra strap, she saw her body in profile. She lowered her hands and looked at herself. What was he talking about? Her breasts were exactly the shape this bra made them. She looked all round, scrutinising herself from several angles. Then she slipped off her bra and looked at herself again. Somehow they did look different, more attractive, now they were free. But she couldn't let men see she didn't wear a bra. Oh dear, there she went again!

She pulled down her briefs and stepped out of them and into the gorgeous soft water. She turned off the tap, a single mixer set at just the right temperature by her doctor adviser, and slipped down, allowing the wet warmth to seep into every part of her body.

As she lay back she noticed that the water-line was shaped by her outline.

'Yes,' she thought for the first time in her life, 'my breasts are as nice as Chris'. A bit smaller, perhaps, but just as good a shape.'

And it pleased her to think such thoughts.

CHAPTER EIGHT

'That's the boathouse.'

'That thing, Peter? It's nearly falling down.'

Being so far from the house and completely out of sight, it tended to be neglected. The wood was bare and rotting in places. It might have made reasonably shelter from a storm but enough daylight chinked through to make it air-conditioned by the elements.

'Race you to it!' Christine set off from the river-bank like a young race-horse and was half way there before Peter had got up top speed. But as she reached the veranda he caught her from behind, his arms going round the flapping hem of the shirt and finding the bareness underneath.

Christine stopped only a moment, turned her head as if to let him kiss her, then pushed the rickety door and went in. Peter followed but she avoided his attempts to renew the embrace.

'No. Work first. Remember your rules! You said you had another idea.'

'I have.'

Again she evaded his clutch. 'I mean for some pictures.'

Peter smiled as he thought of a way of putting his two intentions together. He grasped his camera, and slipped off its cover.

'Right. No more fooling about then. You're working. Er...there, dead centre.'

'Inside here? Is it light enough?'

'Look, my gorgeous -' He lapsed back into the jargon the moment the lens cap was off. 'I'll check the exposure. You expose your lovely self, right?'

'Oh. We're very professional again all of a sudden. Here?'

'Spot on.'

'How do you want me?'

'Absolutely starkers.'

'What?'

'Come on. Don't argue. Take it all off.'

'Just standing here? Like this?'

'Well, I don't mean in Piccadilly Circus. Shirt off, trousers down.'

Christine looked at him hard. Was this a dare? Or was he

really thinking this would make a good shot of something? Or did he just want to strip her and...? Well, there was only one way to find out.

She turned her back on him and undid the three lower buttons holding her shirt round her body.

'What's all the modesty bit? This way round if you don't mind. I want to shoot you as you peel. What I'm after is a strip tease of pictures, get it?'

Christine looked at him, smiled as she imagined a temptress would and began the unbuttoning sequence again.

Click. 'Not so fast.' Click. 'Now the bottom one.' Click. 'Good. Hold it. Now one at a time.'

'What d'you mean, one at a time. There aren't any more.'

'Not buttons, darling...The boobs. Let's have one showing. That's right. That's a beaut. Freeze that.' Peter encircled her breast like an astronaut getting shots of various sides of the moon. Its spherical surface passed across his viewfinder as he circumnavigated without taking the camera from his eye.

'Right. Release Number Two.'

Christine laughed. And her other breast twinned the first one. Peter sucked in air. 'If Eve had boobies like those, no wonder Man's in the mess he's in today.'

Again he clicked. 'Now shirt sleeves off and freeze again.' He had chosen the moment when her hands were behind her, tugging the last of the shirt from her wrists, her breasts thrusting forward and defenceless.

But he didn't take the shot. He moved one side, then the other. Then closed in. He lowered the camera.

'What's the matter then?'

'You.'

Peter dropped his camera onto its safety sling. He moved toward her, and began to caress her with his soft finger tips.

Christine closed her eyes, took in air sharply as he nipped at her. But she didn't complain. This was ecstasy.

Sybil walked quickly along the path through the rhododendrons. She knew it was well past the time Peter needed for a straight forward photo session. And she suspected the boathouse was a possible cause of the delay. As she approached it, she heard Christine yelp in pleasurable agony. She moved stealthily towards the boarded side which was scratched by overhanging trees.

'That hurt, Peter! Don't bite them off.'

Then he kissed her, long but not passionately. At least it didn't seem as passionate as Christine would have liked in her present state. There was a hint of an assumed apology in his eyes. Regret too. But he daren't let himself go while there was work to be done.

'Come on. You're only half ready. Down with the pants, please. Slowly.'

Christine needed no prompting. Her eyes were willing him to do it for her. Her lips were moist, her breathing quickening. She slipped the waist clip and thrust the zip down the flies almost before he got the fist shot in.

'Hang on a minute! Let me get the picture first!'

She stood with her hands on the zip, her arms pressing her breasts together.

Click. 'Now, bring your hands up either side of the zip, to the top. Good. Look at me.'

Christine was serf-like in her obedience. She wished Peter would put his camera down. She wanted to see him look at her as a man should. But he was transfixed with his viewfinder.

They were both oblivious that someone else was looking too. Sybil was peering through a slit in the boards. Her face was contorted with rage and she was fighting to contain herself.

'Lovely.' Click. 'Now, slowly, down to the knees.' Click. 'Right, let 'em go. Drop 'em.' The jeans fell to her ankles. But Peter did not lower his camera. Click. Click. 'Now lift one foot out.' Click. 'Now the other.' Click. 'Now pick them up and dangle them between you boobies.' Christine could have been doing this sort of thing for years. She was still learning - eagerly.

She looked down the jeans. They dropped straight in front of her breasts as if she was trying to be modest. She tried to adjust them, but not to Peter's satisfaction.

Peter came up to her. 'Like this, I mean,' and he draped the two legs on her pelvis. His hand brushed her. She felt a shiver of awakening desire. But the moment passed. He stepped back and aimed his camera.

'Fine. Last one. You've been very good. Hold out the jeans to me. As if offering them.'

Christine did so, willingly. She was really saying visually: 'Here! Have them. I'm happy to be naked with you. For you.'

Click. The final shot was put onto film and, to her delight, Peter took the jeans from her and threw them into a corner. He slung off his cameras, using the pants to cushion them against the ground as he lowered them carefully.

'Is it all over?'

'The photo session, yes.' Peter put his hands on Christine's shoulders. She did not move. He drew his fingers forward and down over her breasts. He cupped the mounds of flesh with his hands. Christine took his chin in her hands and kissed him encouragingly.

So this was how it felt! She'd read about it, thought about it, dreamed it so often, but this was the first time she'd allowed her body to be subservient to a man's whims. She was almost afraid of the lengths her own passions might lead her to once they were aroused. But she couldn't think straight. She didn't want to.

Each time he moved his hands she kissed him, showing her pleasure, inviting him on. His hands wandered, like a blind man trying to read her shape, moving over her body as she moaned in delight.

Sybil could stand no more. She ran back in the direction of the house. She stopped and tried to control her breathing and compose her features.

Christine felt her knees growing weak, as if willing her to lie down. Peter pulled on her thighs to draw her down.

Suddenly he stopped. 'Listen!' From outside Sybil was calling 'Peter! Where are you? How's it going?'

He dashed to a slit in the wall and saw Sybil, apparently walking towards the boathouse for the first time.

Christine was very frustrated by the interruption. 'Don't answer. Maybe she'll go away.'

'She won't. She knows this place.'

Sybil was covering her anger cleverly. She called again: 'Peter! Can you spare a minute darling?'

'Must you?' Christine pleaded unashamedly, making no attempt to put her clothes on. She saw him pulling at his tight trousers. She was excited by the effect she had on him.

'I'll have to go. She'll suspect. Get dressed, for heaven's sake!'

'Why?'

'Because she's my boss. And she knows how long a session should take. There'll be other times.' He kissed her and made to leave. 'I'm as sorry as you are.'

He didn't seem to be. She couldn't have stopped if he hadn't.

Christine heard him call. 'Coming Sybil!'

She lay oblivious of the rotting wood floor, naked bodily and emotionally.

Sybil had turned to stride back to the house and as Peter caught her up, she snapped: 'What d'you think you're playing at, you dirty little lecher?'

'I'm sorry, Sybil. She's so super, I went to town. I've got some great shots. Wait till you see them.'

'That's what you're paid for. To take pictures. Not to indulge yourself in cheap thrills.'

'You can't really blame me! I'm human, you know. That girl's out of this world.'

'I don't need you to tell me. Just keep your pawing hands off her from now on. That's an order.'

Peter detected jealousy.

'So you've got eyes on her yourself. Designs of your own. Well, you can forget that in a great big hurry. She's not only very lovely, very young and very sexy. She's so normal she's unique. thank God!'

'Don't talk to me like that.' Sybil's eyes burned at him like lasers.

'So fire me, then. Too bad.' It was the first time he'd defied her like this. He surprised himself.

Her finger stabbed in his direction.

'I'll do worse than that. I'll make you wish all I had done was fire you.'

Gerald Amberley, watching from his bedroom window, suddenly realised what she was up to. He quickly opened the window and shouted to disturb her before it was too late.

'Sybil!'

He was just in time. Sybil lowered her finger and her eyes weakened, tired from the exertion. Peter did not realise how nearly he'd been in deep trouble. He thought Sybil was flaring into one of her temperamental tirades. But if he'd only known, that wasn't the half of it.

Gerald pretended he was only calling them.

'Sybil. Peter. Come up here, will you? I'd like a word.'

Betty was so soaked with perfumes and soaps and bath-oils that she imagined herself luxuriating in the classic film star scene. She was blissfully unaware that the eye of a decorative dolphin immediately opposite the end of the bath was a fish-eye lens. And on the other side, in Gerald's bedroom, he returned to watch her through it, waiting for the supreme moment when she got out. The fish-eye lens was designed to show the whole picture where Betty would stand to dry herself.

Sensuously, reluctantly, Betty raised herself up. In the fish-eye the glistening wetness highlighted her breasts, and, when she turned to reach a towel, her buttocks. But Gerald quickly closed the false cupboard which hid his viewing position, when there was a knock at the door.

Sybil entered in time to see the frustration on his face as he moved away from the cupboard. She knew what he had been doing.

'What are you peeping at her for? She's not the one I've chosen!'

'Never mind what I'm doing, Sybil. I saw what you were trying to do to Peter just now. I will not have you dabbling in the Black Arts. Not here in my coven. White witchcraft only is my unbreakable rule. I've told you before. This is the last time I'll repeat it.'

Sybil was worried because Peter was coming up the stairs behind her and would shortly come in. So she did not deny his accusation.

'There is another girl, Gerald. She's the one I've chosen for you. The sister.

Peter came in. Sybil was glad to have steered the conversation clear of her spell casting.

'We were just talking about Christina and Betty.'

'Christina's a lovely girl,' said Peter.

'Betty's a lovely girl, too.' Gerald thought of her nude in the bath. 'Delectable.'

'But it's to be Christina.' Sybil was adamant.

'Why shouldn't he use Betty if he wants to?' Peter made the point, but half-heartedly, knowing he was too weak to coerce Sybil.

'I say Christina. I choose the girls, Peter, I've warned you -'

'Sybil!' Gerald cut off her rising anger.

Christine, jeans and shirt clinging skin-tight ran up the staircase and heard the voices coming from Gerald's room. She paused, just past the half-opened door.

First she heard Peter. 'I still don't see why it has to be tonight.'

Then Sybil. 'Because it's Lammas. And it's all arranged.'

'There's to be a full meeting.' Gerald's voice she did not recognise. 'And I shall perform the Third Rite.'

Christine's eye widened. Then the door was closed from inside and she moved on to her own room.

As she entered, a cosseted Betty emerged from the bathroom wrapped in a towel.

'How did it go, Chris?'

Christine tried to be offhand. 'Oh I think it was okay. Peter seemed pleased anyway.'

'Come on then, get changed. It'll be dinner time soon.'

Christine stripped and went into the bathroom.

'Have you met Doctor Amberley yet?' Betty called after her from the dressing table.

Christine shook her head as she washed the day's work from her body. 'No.'

'I have. He's a poppet. And guess what I've found. There's a cellar downstairs. Decorated like some sort of chapel.'

Christine reacted. 'A chapel? What sort of chapel?'

'The funny thing is there's no cross on the altar. Just a dagger and a horrid looking whip. And chains and iron things, and stuffed bats hanging from the ceiling. Gruesome if you think of what must have gone on there.'

Christine's eyes widened. 'Witches' rites. Great!'

'I don't see what's great about it. I found it rather spooky. And I can't believe Doctor Amberley knows about it.'

'Why not? Maybe he's a witch himself. There are male witches you know.' Christine moved out from the shower.

'Doctor Amberley? He's much too nice.'

'They don't all wear pointed hats and ride on broomsticks, silly. There are such things as white witches.'

'Well, if he's got anything to do with it, you can bet he'd not doing anything...nasty. I mean, after all he is a doctor.'

Christine gave a sceptical smile. 'From what I've just heard we're going to find out pretty soon.'

'What have you heard?'

'You'll see. Dry my back, Betty.'

'Oh, Chris, don't be mean! Tell me.' Betty towelled down Christine's spine.

'No.' Christine pretended to be secretive and menacing. 'It's all going to happen. Surprise, surprise.'

'Tell me. Please.'

'And spoil everything?'

'It isn't something...nasty. Is it? I mean, will I like it?'

Christine's win-her-over smile lit up her face.

'How old do we have to be before you trust me. I won't let you down, Betty.'

Christine moved out into the bedroom. Betty followed.

'I still think you might tell me.'

'Come on. It's nearly time for dinner. You might learn more then.'

Mrs Dixon was as friendly a landlady as the girls could have wished for. She had no time to mother them or worry about their comings and goings, as she explained in no uncertain terms to her son.

She opened their bedsitting room door with a master key.

'She told me as they dashed out. There's a note for you on the mantelpiece. See? What did I tell you?'

Johnny had already got the envelope open and begun to read.

'Dear Johnny. By the time you read this, Chris and I will be out in the country. I know we said you and I, and maybe Chris, would do that very thing ourselves, but I suddenly thought I'd better go with Chris and see she didn't get mixed up in anything shady. You said there's no safety in numbers, but it must help a bit and I didn't fancy her going off out in the blue just like that. You never know, do you?'

Johnny felt his mother straining to read over his shoulder. He moved out of range.

'Don't be so nosy, Ma. Didn't she say where they were going?'

Mrs Dixon shrugged good-humouredly.

'No. Don't she say in her letter? Come to think of it, maybe they didn't know themselves.'

'She said she'd ring here and leave a number where I could call her.'

'Been no call yet. But you know what girls are today. Better than I do no doubt!'

'Crazy kids!'

Johnny finished reading Betty's note. 'Sorry about all this, Johnny. If you can come down on Sunday, super. If not, see you Monday. any time you say. Lots of love. Betty.' He put it back in the envelope and then in his pocket. He saw Sybil's studio card on the mantelpiece.

'This where Christine got the job?'

'Blessed if I know. They didn't tell me nothing. They were pretty excited, that's for sure.'

Johnny put the card in his pocket with the note. He made for the front door, frowning. His mother followed him out and locked the girls' door behind them.

'I just hope she remembers to ring me, that's all.'

'D'you think those two can't look after themselves, then?'

This was not said unkindly.

'I'd just like to know they're all right, that's all. Well, I must be off!'

'You going again so soon?'

He gave her a peck on the cheek.

'Sorry Mum, I promised Abby I'd pick her up at the studio.'

She wagged an admonitory finger at him. 'You be careful, Johnny. Playing around with that Abby and running after this kid. She's little more than a child - the type that'll get hurt.'

'Not if I can help it. Anyway, you know you're my favourite girl.' A cheeky grin, a wave and he was gone.

Gerald Amberley knew how to lay on a dinner-party. And how to use the setting. The dinning-room glowed from a row of candle-flames flickering in single candelabra down the centre of the mahogany table.

Gerald raised his long-stemmed glass, red with a chateau bottled wine.

'I wish to propose a toast. To our charming visitors.' He held his glass to his left, where Christine smiled radiantly, her eyes flashing reflections of the tiny flames. 'Christine.' Christine matched her glass to his. Then he held his glass to his right. 'Betty.' The simple ritual was repeated. Sybil, from the other end of the table, and Peter, across from Christine, joined in the toasts.

'Christine. Betty.'

It had been a meal the girls would always remember. Christine talked animatedly throughout about her modelling ambitions, bringing into her conversation a rag-bag of background information she had religiously culled from magazines and Sunday paper gossip columns. Gerald had listened courteously, seemingly attentive. Betty had said little, wondering when she was going to get some idea of what might happen. Peter was in a sullen mood, although Christine was too elated to notice his lowering expression across the table. To watch this gorgeous girl - so near and yet so far - was his idea of medieval torture.

Sybil was in an ideal position to interject the odd comment and yet observe the cool polished way Gerald was gaining absolute confidence of both twins.

Gerald played down the meal. 'I hope you don't find the way I entertain too formal.'

'No,' Christine eulogised, 'it's super. We're having a marvellous time!'

'I want you to feel completely at home here. That you can go anywhere you wish, do anything you have a mind to.'

Betty giggled, her tongue beginning to be loosened by the wines. 'Home was never like this, was it, Chris? It feels like Christmas, all these candles and a dinner like that.'

'Not Christmas,' Sybil only came in when Christine's chatter flagged momentarily. Now she corrected Betty in a deliberate tone of voice. 'It's Lammas.'

Gerald gave her a sharp look from under his brows. 'Yes,' he explained, 'we celebrate Lammas tonight. Have you ever heard of Lammas?'

Christine showed enthusiasm. 'It's a witches' festival, isn't it?'

Gerald smiled at her interest. 'That is exactly how we celebrate it.'

'In the chapel under here?'

There was a moments silence. Christine realised her impetuous reply had given Betty's visit way, but she had no reason to believe it would cause adverse reaction. Betty looked down at the table, wondering what Gerald would say when he found out about the chapel. Peter and Sybil looked at Gerald but he remained calm, not exchanging any informative glances with them.

'Of course, that is what the chapel is for. I didn't know you'd been down yet?'

'Oh, I haven't. Betty found it.'

'I heard Lucifer asking to get in at the door. I thought it was just a cellar. So I let him in. I didn't know it was a chapel. Not till I looked in, I mean.'

Gerald patted Betty's hand on the table. 'That's all right, my dear. There's nothing secret about it. Not as far as you are concerned. I would have shown it to you.'

Christine could hardly wait. 'When? It sounds fascinating.'

Betty was looking at Gerald, still not understanding.

'Then, you are a...witch?'

Sybil looked at Gerald again, but he adjudged the time was

right to admit it. His voice was calm, reassuring. 'I am. Don't be shocked, Betty. I'm a white witch.'

'I'm not shocked - not exactly. Just...well, I've never met a witch before and I'd no idea...It's difficult to believe.'

Gerald removed his hand, sat back in his chair to show he was quite at ease. 'Yet if you'd just learned I was...say, a Catholic or...a Jew...or a Moslem, you wouldn't find that difficult to believe? Witchcraft is a religion, after all. My religion. Why is it difficult to believe I'm a witch then?'

Betty was still confused. 'Witchcraft is a religion?'

'One of the oldest. Perhaps the very oldest. Nobody knows.'

Christine jumped in. 'She thinks you worship the Devil and practise evil.'

Gerald smiled, but adopted an air of injured innocence. 'Emphatically not. In fact, quite the contrary. My coven is dedicated to practising white witchcraft. We try, in our own...special...witchcraft ways...to do good by it.' He looked significantly at Sybil who was watching Christine's reactions.

'You mean - faith healing, that sort of thing?'

'Faith healing comes within our practices, of course. We exist on a very simple level really. For friendship and...' He looked at Betty and slightly raised his glass to her. 'And to give pleasure where we can.'

If Christine's next excited question had not come treading hard on Gerald's last words, a snort of disgust would have been heard, and Peter was the perpetrator.

Christine's eyes were alight in anticipation. 'Are we going to visit your chapel soon? Am I the only one here who hasn't seen it?'

Gerald looked at the others. 'You are. We'll put that right this very moment, shall we? While they have coffee. Or would you prefer to wait...?'

Gerald shot back the bolt in the big cellar door. Christine couldn't wait for him to usher her in. She went ahead. Gerald smiled as he followed. This was going to be so easy he could hardly credit it.

The chapel was now lit by candles which threw wavering shadows of the bats on to the ceiling, of chains on to the stone walls, of the altar on to the dais. The dagger and scourge were on the altar as Betty had said. But Christine found it far more exciting than she even imagined she would. The place had an atmosphere which seemed to soak right inside her, into the marrow of her bones. She went up to the altar and stood facing it as if it were a cathedral with a reredos of great beauty. It was the way she'd looked at the moon when they were hitching a lift to London.

'How do I become a witch?'

Gerald came from behind her and stepped up on to the dais, turning to look down at her. 'First you must indicate you have the true desire.'

'I have. I felt it. The moment we came in.'

Gerald put out his hands and rested them on her shoulders. She nearly jumped as she felt a vibration from his touch shoot down her spine. Then, as the pressure from his hands increased, she knelt involuntarily. He tilted her face and she saw his eyes change, become mystical. There were lovely eyes.

He placed both hands on her head very gently, then slowly forced it down. Nothing was said; there was no need. She remained in this abject position for a few moments, feeling serene, as if some additional force was flowing into her very being. Then Gerald took his hands from her head and raised her. One hand went gently under her chin and their gaze met again. She was smiling, but tears of emotion were welling inside her shining eyes.

'What did you feel?'

'Beautiful vibrations, like an electric shock.'

'You are very receptive. Very receptive indeed. I was transmitting strength. Some people don't feel anything at all.'

'Does it mean I can be a witch?'

'Some people are born to be witches. Only a very few. You, Christina, are one of them.'

Christine could hardly believe her good fortune.

Sybil appeared at the door. 'We have a lot to prepare, Gerald.'

'I know.' There was a trace of annoyance in his voice at the interruption.

'For tonight? Can I join in?' Christine pleaded.

'There will come a moment when you'll hear the call. Not before.'

'Tonight? Oh, please make it tonight.'

'The time will come when it must come.'

'How will I know?'

'You will know. Be patient. And be ready. I think you and your sister should have an early night.'

Christine's face registered disappointment, but Gerald insisted.

'Particularly Betty. She needs a good rest after the shock of her fall. I'll make her one of my herb drinks. Now go to her.'

Christine looked at Sybil who smiled and side-stepped for her to leave. Reluctantly Christine went.

Sybil closed the door behind her. 'That girl's the best I've found yet.'

'I agree. Quite amazing.'

'But don't think you're taking her over completely. I found her. And I retain an interest in her.' Sybil spoke as if Christine were a piece of property.

'True, Sybil. But why so angry about it?'

'Because young Peter's got hot pants and it's no use you going through your routine with her if you send her off to be alone with him upstairs. We'd better get back. You can't trust that boy an inch.'

'Now wait a moment! I want nothing to do with your little schemes, but I must have an understanding there is to be no more meddling with Black spells. Is that clear?'

Sybil was angry. 'Look, I don't interfere in your business. Don't interfere in mine. You're charging the locals for membership of your club here. I'm nobody's fool, Gerald.'

'What are you on about?'

'Don't tell me you make enough to keep up the way you live in this place from writing your stuffy old books. I know you've got a nice little earner on the side.'

With this parting shot Sybil turned and made for the door. But Gerald strode after her, and took her arm to spin her round to face him.

'Yes, it takes more money than my "stuffy" books bring in. Thank you for that kind compliment. But I haven't noticed you complaining about my hospitality.'

Sybil immediately regretted the insult to his work; she know how sensitive he was about his ability.

'I'm sorry Gerald. I didn't mean that, about your writing. I'm a bit edgy. I've my work cut out keeping Peter's hands off our new find.'

'I agree. There's no purpose served in a slagging match. I accept your apology. That girl is going to be very good.'

Sybil inclined her head graciously. 'Just as long as you remember, Gerald, that I found her - for myself as well as for you.'

'I wonder if you know exactly what you have found?'

Sybil went without catching the full implication of his words. Gerald remained absolutely motionless, staring at the altar. There was a strange, thoughtful expression on his face.

Johnny was standing beside the parked Jaguar talking to Jock MacNair of Photopress News. Jock had a nervous habit of checking the focus setting of his camera nearly every time he spoke. From the grim look on Johnny's face, what he had just heard Jock say was not to his liking.

'You serious?' he asked. 'Straight up?'

'Serious? I don't know a model who isn't ready to run a mile from her. If they can get enough jobs elsewhere. Of course, sometimes they have no choice. But they have to watch it.'

'Bad as that?' Johnny could hardly believe it.

'They say they wear protective clothing at the Sybil Waite Studio. Armour-plated panties.' Jock laughed.

'You're laying it on a bit thick.'

'I'm not laying anything on. What're you so worried about? She's not interested in fellers. That's for sure.'

'A friend of mine's gone off for the weekend with her.'

'Girlfriend?'

'Sort of. Yeah.'

'Well, if you haven't taught her the facts of life, she'll learn 'em now...and fast!'

They looked across to the TV studio doors where the groups of teen-kids began to agitate their heads and their autograph books.

'Ah well,' Jock moved off towards them. 'Takes all kinds. Cheerio, Johnny.'

Studio officials tried to make a way through the crowd. There was no mistaking the lissom and strikingly beautiful Abby Drake. Her hair sparkled with festoons of diamonds, her dress flashed silver and gold from under the sable coat thrown round her shoulders.

She smiled at the kids, her teeth so white against her soft coffee coloured skin they looked artificial. Her Negroid nostrils flared as she was jostled.

'Now don't get rough, kids, you'll spoil my writing. Never was much good at school!'

Good humouredly she signed all the way to the car.

Jock followed, flashing his strobe-light time after time.

'One before you get in, Miss Drake,' asked Jock and she

obliged. A brief nod to Johnny acknowledged his presence.

Johnny closed the door, cutting off the outstretched unsigned books, and went round to the driver's seat. He gunned the Jag's cylinders but looked tight-lipped as he released the brake and moved off smoothly.

Abby flopped her head back.

'Johnny remind me to refuse any more chat appearances on that little squit's show.'

'You told me to last time. And I did.'

'Too late. Remind me before I commit myself next time. He can make the most innocent answers sound like farmyard muck.

'That's what they pay him for.'

'Well, it's not going to be what they pay me for.'

'Straight home?' Johnny was too wrapped up in his own worries to be sympathetic.

A shaft of moonlight streamed into the bedroom. It had just caught Betty's face, but she slept on like a babe. Whatever had been in that herb drink, it worked like a charm. In contrast Christine was hot and restless. Every time she closed her eyes she found herself thinking of the chapel, going through her idea of what took place during a ceremony. She could see Gerald in some sort of robes, raising his hands, to a background of incomprehensible incantations. Then suddenly the voices ceased and lights flashed. Gerald's hands were lowered as he lowered them earlier on her shoulders. She still felt them, the energies pouring into her. It built and built until she felt she must burst.

Suddenly she sat bolt upright, trying to shake the imagery out of her mind. If she went on like this, she'd get no sleep at all and look a right old mess in the morning.

The silence of the night was very quietly punctuated by a rhythmic pulsing. At first she thought it was her own heart, but when she strained to listen, it was identifiable as a muffled drumbeat. This was not in her imagination. It came from somewhere in the house.

At first curious, and not realising she was being drawn to the sound, she tiptoed barefoot to the door, the moonlight making her night-dress diaphanous.

From the landing the beat sounded more clearly. Behind it now she could hear a faint chanting.

She looked back at Betty in deep sleep. Christine quietly closed the door. She padded across the landing and glided silently down the staircase. She was not surprised to find the sounds came from the cellar door. As she opened it, she stopped. Her nostrils dilated as she sniffed. It was an acrid scent, incense or burning joss sticks. She found it heady and exciting.

Her bare feet didn't register the cold stone of the steps. She was intent on reaching the chapel, to see the ceremony.

The big door was not fastened and her slight push caused it to swing open, disclosing the entire scene. Her eyes widened, her jaw dropped. She stood enthralled.

Gerald faced a group of people in a circle. Backed by the altar and the stone wall flickering with candlelight, he wore a dramatic scarlet robe and hood, looking like the High Priest for a very select order of Monks.

His hands were clasped, his head was bowed as if in prayer. Sybil, similarly attired, stood beside him but slightly behind.

Of the others, Christine recognised only the horsewoman who had nearly galloped into them on the river bank. If Betty had been there, she could have identified the milkman and the Colonel also.

But most of the circle were young men and girls, all dressed in monk-like robes of pure white material. They swayed in unison with Gerald and Sybil.

Then Christine saw Peter standing slightly apart. He was not completely absorbed like the others and there was a reluctance about his demeanour. But everyone was so swept up in the ceremony that the intruder in the doorway went unnoticed.

At a sign from Gerald, the horsewoman walked to the centre of the circle. Sybil took the scourge from the altar and moved into position beside him. The circle closed again and continued swaying. The horsewoman looked into Gerald's eyes. She gave a smile of deep gratitude.

Her hands met slowly at her throat and grasped the ends of the cord gathering her robe. As she pulled, the cloak began to slip off her shoulders and down her body. She stood, still looking at Gerald, naked and still. Christine noted that her

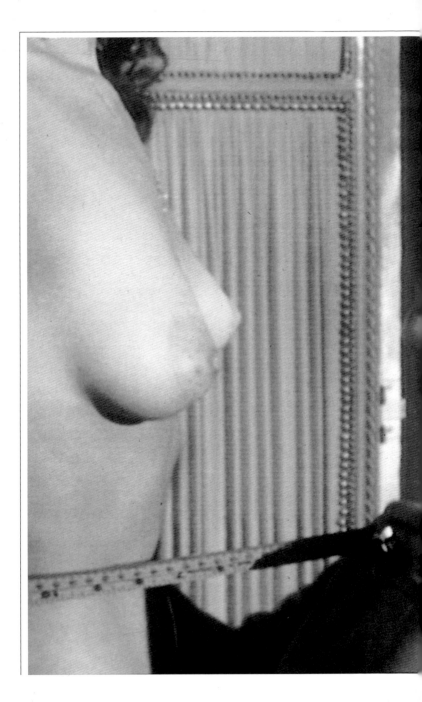

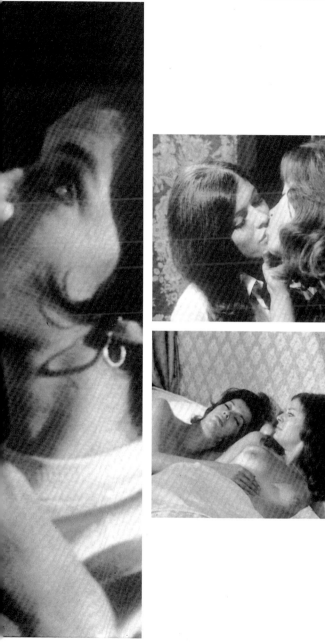

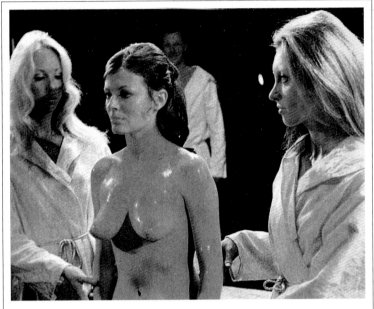

Cast:
Ann Michelle — Christine
Vicky Michelle — Betty
Keith Buckley — Johnny
Patricia Haines — Sybil Waite
James Chase — Peter
Paula Wright — Mrs. Wendell
Christopher Strain — The Milkman
Esme Smythe — The Horse Women
Garth Watkins — The Colonel
Neil Hallet — Gerald Amberley
Helen Downing — Abby Darke
Peter Halliday — The Club Manager
and
**Jenny Klimgnan, Maria Coyne, Sheila Sands, Steve Peters
Prudence Drage, Susan Morrall, David Graham**

Director: Ray Austin
Producer: Ralph Solomons
Written by Klaus Vogel
Editor: Philip Barnike
Director of Photograhpy
Theme song 'You Go Your Way' Music: Ted Dicks
Lyric by Hazel Adair Sung by Helen Downing
Music conducted by Burnell Whibley
DIRECTED BY RAY AUSTIN

breasts, though as full as her own, hung down. It was the body of a woman who had given birth to children.

The women sank slowly to her knees, then grovelled, putting her hands either side of his feet and kissing each of his toes in turn. Gerald stood motionless except for a slightly outstretched hand into which Sybil now put the leather-covered handle of the scourge.

Gerald grasped it, whisked the thongs in the air and brought them down on the woman's bare back, synchronising the lashes with the drum beats.

The circle continued to sway as the thongs whipped across her shoulders, her buttocks and sometimes round her body to flay her breasts. She seemed to turn into these strokes instead of trying to protect the more sensitive parts of her body.

Then Gerald held the scourge high in the air, whirling the thongs round in the opposite direction to the circle, creating an eerie whistling sound.

The woman rose, her eyes glistening at Gerald. He lowered the scourge and she kissed the thongs. Then she clutched them into her breasts, slowly walked out through the circle and replaced the torture instrument on the altar as if it were sacred.

Christine was fascinated, her breasts heaving with excitement. She wished she dare join the circle but was afraid her presence might stop the ceremony if she were discovered.

Now a red-haired girl came forward to stand before Gerald. Her hands went up to the drawstring of her robe but she paused, suddenly unable to bring herself to disrobe. Gerald smiled at her and nodded encouragingly. Her face showed the inner struggle as she wanted to, but could not. At a slight sign from Sybil, two men came from the circle and took her arms from the strings and held them outstretched. The girl's eyes showed her fear but she did not murmur. Christine realised that she had seen her somewhere before. Then it flashed. She was one of the girls who'd posed for the big nude mural behind Sybil's desk in her studio. So it couldn't be disrobing that scared her. What then? Christine was impatient to see.

Gerald stretched out a hand and slowly took hold of the girl's drawstring. She bit her lip, her face was white. Her eyes pleaded with him to treat her gently, but she made no attempt to resist. Christine felt she could have done, if she really wanted it. It reminded her of Peter's biting her. It hurt but she could not stop him. It was a marvellous feeling.

As if filmed in slow-motion, Gerald imperceptibly pulled on the string. And as the gathered robe opened, it fell from her neck to her shoulders, her forcibly extended arms preventing it dropping further. The men lowered her hands to her sides. For a moment, it seemed she would make a grab for a robe, but then it fell to her feet.

The naked girl closed her eyes. Sybil advanced with a chalice of warm oil and anointed her, on the forehead, on her back, and over her breasts, smoothing in the oil with a caressing hand. Then Sybil knelt and began to work upwards from her feet.

The girl bit her lip hard, swayed, and then recovered. Christine saw the oiled breasts glowing in the candlelight. Oh, if only they were hers, they would look even better!

Gerald raised his hands over the glistening figure in a sign of blessing.

Sybil put down the chalice, and intoned: 'The Fivefold Kiss.' The circle echoed; 'The Fivefold Kiss.'

Gerald came close to the girl and put his hands behind her shoulders. Then he bent forward and kissed her left ear.

'One,' the circle intoned.

He kissed the other ear.

'Two.'

He kissed her on the mouth. The girl remained like a slender statue, passive, submissive, resigned.

'Three.'

Now he lowered himself to his knees, his hands sliding down her sides simultaneously. He kissed her navel. 'Four!' echoed round the chapel and it seemed as if the coven all leant forward slightly in anticipation of what was to come.

Christine became bolder. In all this time nobody had noticed her. She had stepped forward a pace or two involuntarily, anxious not to miss the look in the girl's eyes. Was she right in thinking the colour was coming back to her cheeks? She knew how she would feel if Gerald were kissing her. Erotic sensations flooded through her at the sight of Gerald's mouth sinking lower down the girl's abdomen.

'Five!' The chant was at the exact moment of the fifth kiss.

It was like an ecstatic gasp. Now two girls broke the circle and stood behind Gerald as he rose again. They pulled at his robe and revealed him naked, too.

Gerald had the figure of an athlete, his taut muscles etched on his chest, his stomach flat, his legs strong.

The girl stood transfixed as Gerald moved closer to her until there was no space between their bodies. His arms went round her and he began to sway to the beat rhythm. Her body moved in unison with his, without a volition of its own. The others circled round, chanting and murmuring.

Now the drum beats stopped. Christine was suddenly aware of the drummer tucked away in the corner. Now he began a roll on his bongo, quietly at first but imperceptibly growing. It was a signal for the same two men to come forward and take the girl from Gerald. They carried her limp body on to the altar, where she was carefully laid like a sacrificial gift to the gods.

Sybil had taken the ceremonial dagger and now offered it s handle to Gerald. He grasped it and withdrew a two-edged blade from the scabbard. Even from where Christine watched, it looked very sharp. It was, if only she knew, honed to a fine point.

Gerald mounted the dais and approached the altar. He surveyed the girl from head to feet. Her eyes were mesmerised by the dagger as he raised it double-handed high over his head. The drum roll was now reaching an ear-splitting crescendo. Gerald seemed to be measuring the distance from her, lining up his stance so that the dagger's point would meet her body at its precise target. Christine knew she mustn't scream or she would be discovered. She must not interrupt the ceremony. But her eagerness had brought her another involuntary pace forward.

The drum roll reached a crescendo and then suddenly ceased. In this unbearable moment of silence, Gerald drew back his hands that final extra inch, which signified he was about to plunge the blade down. Nobody moved. Christine could hear the soft rustle of her night-dress as her breasts rose and fell beneath it. She realised she was putting herself in the girl's place. She felt terrified and elated at the same time.

But the girl on the altar was now in repose, as if she had

been drained of all emotion. She lay very still on her back, feet together, her eyes fixed on the point of the blade. Gerald's biceps bulged as he gripped the dagger and judged the arc it was about to describe to its target below.

Christine suddenly heard herself whisper an half-strangled 'No!'

Everyone heard it. They all turned, horrified at the intrusion. Christine, her hand to her mouth, her body quivering, was framed just inside the doorway.

'Don't break the circle!' Gerald's commanding voice was sharp, but calm.

He smiled at Christine across the chapel and invited her quietly: 'Come.'

Christine was drawn inexorably to him. If it meant walking across a bed of nails, she would have kept on the straight line taking her to Gerald. She was unaware that Peter put up a restraining hand, but realising it was ineffective, he lowered it with resignation.

Gerald waited for her to reach the dais.

'You wish to join us?'

'Please.'

Sybil's eyes gleamed.

Gerald tested Christine. 'But you disapprove of our rites? Or so it seemed.'

'Oh no! I was just too...excited. I didn't mean to stop you.'

'Then we will continue.'

Christine's head swirled. Impulsively she moved forward. 'Let it be me - please, let it be me!'

She bared herself for the knife. Gerald and Sybil were the only two on the altar dais and their eyes revelled in their privileged front row view.

Gerald whispered 'Kneel!' and she sank into a supplicant position, her heels pressing into her buttocks. Again he raised the dagger high over his head and shifted his stance to measure his aim.

Christine looked up, ignoring the dagger, her eyes on his, unflinching, unafraid. Gerald needed no silent pause as he did with the other girl. The blade flashed in the candlelight as it plunged down. It was a stroke judged to a hairsbreadth accuracy, to a degree impossible by a man less fit, less firmly implanted on the balls of his feet, less in control of his bodily functions under such emotional stress.

Christine's life was not in danger. The blade swept through the deep valley between her breasts. She felt its steely cold against the inner sides of the curves. It excited her as Peter's fingers did. The skill of Gerald's marksmanship was such that the point of the blade made a hairline incision an inch long, so superficial that only a thin red line of blood rose and congealed on her scratched skin.

On the altar, the girl cried out in a hoarse whisper. She drew a finger down between her breasts. When she took it away she bore a red weal to match Christine's bloodmark.

Gerald's face was triumphantly glowing. He threw the dagger aside and raised Christine to her feet. The blade snapped off as it clattered skidding across the stone floor. As if he had expected this unusual occurrence, Gerald pronounced: 'That instrument will never be used in ceremony again.'

Christine's eyes shone as he kissed her full on the mouth. 'Am I a witch now?' she whispered as their lips parted.

'That was the First Rite. You still have to go through the full initiation ceremony.'

'When? When?'

'Again I can only say to you - you will know the right moment. Exactly where to go and what you must do.'

Sybil had brought a silver chalice and Gerald offered it to Christine. 'Drink. In celebration.'

Christine drank. The bitter liquid kissed the dryness inside her mouth, its taste sharply defined and yet indescribable. As she handed the chalice back to Gerald she felt the cool frills of her night-gown as it was lowered over her head. It fell back over her body with the help of two male members of the circle. Even this, Christine found exciting. She had never been publicly naked before, and she had never been dressed by men, even in private. These new experiences were wonderful, this was living in a way she had never dreamed could be so stimulating.

The first person to drink from the chalice after her was Sybil. Christine saw her eyes piercing over the rim of the silver cup straight into her own.

Gerald put his hands on Christine's shoulders. Even though he had been robed again this gesture was still as exciting. But her heart slowed with disappointment as he ordered: 'You must leave us now.'

Christine shook her head. But Gerald insisted.

'What follows now is not for you, not until you are initiated. Rest. And be ready for that supreme moment when it comes.'

He turned to face the door and she began to walk, reluctance in her steps. She was still in a dream world. Peter made a move towards her but Sybil had been waiting for this. She gripped his wrist and restrained him. Peter had not the courage to shake free and follow Christine. He wished he had.

'You were told not to break the circle,' she whispered fiercely.

Peter swung round on her, angrily, only to meet a reproving look from Gerald too. He heard the big door close and turned to see Christine had gone.

Betty had been restless ever since the moonlight moved on, leaving her face in shadow. She had tossed from one side to the other until the bed-clothes had bunched into a heap at the foot of the bed. Now she lay almost naked, and a sudden chilled breeze combined with the sound of Christine opening the door brought sudden consciousness. She sat up.

'Who is it?'

'Me.' Christine closed the door behind her.

Betty sighed with relief. 'Chris! Where on earth have you been? What time is it?'

'I don't know. Time doesn't seem to mean anything.' Christine sat on the bed, took Betty's hand.

'When the door opened I got a fright. I thought you were in bed.'

'I know.'

Christine rolled into the bed beside her and pulled up the sheets and blankets.

Betty felt the glow of Christine's body. 'You're warm.'

'There's nothing to be afraid of, Betty. Just the opposite. I have a marvellous feeling...I can't just explain it. But I know something wonderful's going to happen to us. The world...it's going to open up for us. You'll see.'

'Funny thing. I'm never frightened when you're with me. I don't worry at all.'

'That's right.' Christine's arms went round her and they lay cuddled together. 'You stick with me, I'll make it go right. For both of us.'

The Sybil Waite Studio was dark and still. Only a car engine carrying some night-owls along the King's Road disturbed the silence. The torch that focused on Miss Fletcher's desk revealed nothing of interest. Then its beam was directed on the door marked Private.

The torch-bearer moved silently; he tried the handle. The door gave and the beam swung round Sybil's studio. As soon as it verified there were no tell-tale windows, it searched for a light switch. The hand that switched it on was Johnny Dixon's. He was wearing driving gloves and creeper shoes as any real burglar might have done.

The sudden illumination of the nude murals had a momentary impact on him. But Johnny's mood was too grim to allow his mind to dwell on eroticism. The other pictures drew no more than a cursory glance, except to confirm Jock's nasty image of Sybil Waite. The desk interested him more. He tried the drawers. They were all locked and he sighed in exasperation.

He was about to force the top one when he noticed Sybil's large diary in front of him. He opened it and turned the pages to the relevant Sunday. The weekend had a diagonal line scored across it and one word covered both days. 'Wychwold.'

Christine couldn't sleep. The events of the night had excited her so much that she was reliving them over and over again. Betty was in deep sleep and when Christine disengaged her arms from around her gently, she showed no sign of stirring.

Christine felt compelled to get up. She just couldn't stay in bed. She found that the room gave her an overbearing feeling of claustrophobia. Slowly, calmly, as if sleep-walking, she moved out onto the landing and down the staircase. She felt that even the high lofted hall was not open enough and she moved outside, happier to have the sky above her, the open air, cool but soft, teasing her under her night-gown. The gardens were an idyllic setting, lit by moonlight and festooned with stars.

On impulse she began to run across the lawns, into the woods and up the hillside through the bracken. Her bare feet pounded the earth to the same rhythmic beat that throbbed throughout the ceremony in the chapel. She couldn't tell whether it was drumming in her ears in reality, or in her memory.

Suddenly she crested the hill and the Druids' stones stood erect, silhouetted against the dark blue sky. In amongst them, the assembly from the chapel were dancing gracefully, joyously, their white robes tinged steel-blue by the moon. Christine was not surprised. Somehow she expected to find them there. But this time she was no interloper. Two members detached themselves from the circle and in one continuous movement took her hands and drew her into the dance. The rhythms grew gradually wilder, more erotic. She felt it building up to a climax. She found herself in the centre of the circle, each dancer, in turn, moved in to embrace her, twirl and move back into the circle.

The spinning and whirling in this strange light made her feel dizzy and when all the white figures began to spin in towards her she fell limply to the ground. But she had not fainted. If anything, she felt more acutely aware then ever before in her life.

Gerald was immediately beside her, looking deep into her eyes. He smiled in triumph to see they were glazed. He raised his hands to the stars and the dancing stopped. The figures stood motionless, like statues, as Gerald dropped to his knees beside Christine's body as if in prayer.

When he raised himself up, two young men came forward and picked Christine up. Slowly, they carried her as they did the girl in the chapel and placed her on a huge stone slab in the centre of the circle of stones.

Sybil's eyes gleamed intensely as she approached the rude altar with a chalice of oil. Two girls walked ahead of her and disrobed Christine.

She stirred as if coming out of sleep as they raised her body to draw the night-dress up under her buttocks, but she made no sign of resistance. Then they prepared her for complete anointing. Sybil stood ready, impatient to spread the oil on the inert body.

Christine lay flat on her back in the very centre of the stone. Her arms were stretched out crucifix fashion, a lighted black candle was place in each hand. She gripped them tightly, holding them erect. Her wide-open eyes, reflecting the flickering flames, were luminous and mystical.

She realised that although her body seemed no longer under her control, and she could not run away if she wanted to - which she didn't - her mind was so crystal-clear that she sensed all that was about to happen. As Sybil put out her hand, cupped with oil, she almost felt its unctuous caress before it touched her. And she noticed, for the first time, a blood-red birthmark on the inside of Sybil's wrist. It had a strange shape, evil-looking, in a way Christine couldn't explain. It reminded her of something and she racked her memory to place it. But without success. Her awareness was so much of the here and now that the past and future had no place on her consciousness.

These thoughts were drowned by sensual emotions as Sybil anointed her from her forehead downwards. She lingered lovingly over her body.

The rhythm began to build to a climax. Gerald stepped forward to the foot of the slab. The girls stripped him of his robe but this time their frenzy was in significant contrast to the symbolic ceremony in the chapel. The dancers were now writhing, gyrating and throwing off their robes. Sybil had anointed Christine until every part of her was glistening with oil. Now she ran to the head of the slab and she too threw off her robe. She stretched her hands forward like antennae sensing for vibrations.

Christine could only see the moon and stars until Gerald mounted the stone slab. His naked body towered into her view as he placed his feet between hers. But she did not move, her arms and legs stayed star-shaped; her hands gripped the candles tighter.

A single cloud had crept across the dark sky and passed over the moon. As the light dimmed she saw Gerald plunging down towards her. Her body was ready to receive him and, with a cry of anguish, took him in.

Only now did she close her eyes. She no longer had to see. She could feel. Everything.

The morning sun was well up when Christine awoke. She turned on her back to find the ceiling was different from the one in her room. Then she realised she was in a double-bed, not with Betty, but Sybil.

Sybil was asleep but felt the movement and turned towards her. Her bare arms came across Christine just as she was about to slide out of the bedclothes.

Christine was desperately trying to remember just what had happened. The memory was as vague now as the reality had been so sharp. If she had wakened in her own bed, she would have accepted that she had been dreaming. It was all so dreamlike, haunting her mind, none of it clear or definite. Yet her body ached to remind her of the experience she had been through. That was not imaginary. She felt bruised and tender. Her cheeks flushed as she realised the cause of it. But she was not ashamed, rather she was triumphant. If this really had happened then she had put childhood behind her forever. Now she was a woman.

She took hold of Sybil's wrist gently to get free and suddenly saw the birthmark. This she did remember now. She examined it closely. It reminded her of something. But what? Something not long ago? Something...But what? Still her memory failed her.

Somehow she shrank back from touching the ugly patch. She carefully moved the encircling arm, whilst Sybil slept on, only murmuring in dreamy protest. Once free, Christine slipped out of the bed. Her night-dress lay on the floor; she drew it on and went quietly out of the room.

Johnny stopped the Jaguar at a small wooden signpost. The lettering had not been repainted for years but he could just make out 'Wychwold 2' in the early sunlight. He turned off the country road into the lane indicated.

Betty brushed her hair at the dressing table. 'I slept like a log, Chris. Apart from when you came back from getting a drink I don't remember a thing until you shook me. Whatever Doctor Amberley put in that drink, I don't know.'

'You can bet it wasn't drugs, that's for certain.'

'Why not? He's a doctor.'

'Yes, but a very special sort of doctor. He told me he'd mix you a herb drink.'

'Well, some doctors use herbs.'

'Betty, how d'you know he's a doctor?'

'Because he told me. And I could tell from the things he...things he said. The way he does things.'

Christine looked out of the window, stretched happily. 'He's no ordinary doctor, that's for sure.'

'What makes you say that?'

Christine asked herself the same question. 'I don't know. I just feel he isn't.'

Betty shrugged. There was something more important on

her mind. 'I hope Johnny phones soon.'

'Did you give this number to his Mum?'

'Just before dinner last night. She said he'd been round but went out again straight away. He seemed worried. He was going to ring back later.'

'Then he'll be on to you, if he's as keen as he makes out he is. Stop worrying.'

'I'm not worrying. Just...I want to see him. Now don't you tell him that.'

'I won't.'

The sun made the lawns look greener than Christine could ever remember seeing grass before. 'It's a fabulous morning.' She saw Peter appear from the house and move off in the direction of the woods. He seemed disconsolate, kicking moodily at a stone on the path.

Christine turned from the window and made straight for the door, announcing, 'I'm going out,' without pausing.

In the next bedroom, Sybil awoke. A sudden turn of the head and she discovered the empty space beside her. A frown creased her brow. She was disappointed; she had especially wished to see Christine's awakening this morning. To be the one to show her the delights in store now that she had been initiated. Well, there'd be other chances later on.

She sighed and dragged herself out of bed reluctantly. It would have been good to lie in after last night. But Christine was awake and mustn't be left to her own devices. She'd probably be in her own room now, dressing. Sybil pulled on her negligee as she looked out of the window for her first sight of the day. She saw Peter moving towards the woods and then Christine running through the garden in the same direction, her hair flying carefree like a slipstream.

Sybil's face flamed with vicious intent.

Peter flopped down on the grass, his back propped against a Druid's stone. Somehow in sunlight the slabs seemed to have lost their mystique. Christine came running up and dropped down beside him. She stretched her arms behind her head and arched her back in the sheer joy of new-found life.

She saw Peter looking despondent and reached up to pull his

head towards her. 'Why so miserable?'

Peter could only say 'Chris...' before she cut off her explanation with a kiss. She let her lips part. They locked together, his tongue thrusting into her mouth, her lips holding it tight.

When they broke, she held her cheek against his and murmured: 'Peter - last night? Up here? Was it you? Tell me it was. Please.'

He could tell from the urgency in her voice that she was hoping he'd say yes. But he was incredulous. 'Don't you know, Christine? Honestly?'

'It's like a dream. A weird and yet wonderful dream. But I can't remember any of it for certain - not clearly.'

Peter grew angry. 'He hypnotised you. Must have. If you don't know, he must have.'

'Gerald? It was Gerald then?'

'Bloody Gerald. He's done it before. I don't understand it, but I've seen him. The High Priest. The High Priest always performs the Initiation. Or the High Priestess.' He beat his fist on the ground until it grew red, as angry as he was.

She kissed him, this time very gently and relaxed. He responded and then she broke away. 'See? This is what matters, isn't it?'

Peter got up and looked down towards the river. Christine joined him and took his hand as they began to descend the steep path to the bank,

'One thing I do know. I am a witch. And now I can please myself.'

'Chris, you worry me when you say things like that. I don't think you've any idea what you've got yourself into. I should have warned you. I did try, but I should have insisted. I don't seem to be able to stand up to them.'

'It wouldn't have made any difference. So don't blame yourself.'

'I thought this ceremonial stuff a bit larky when I first got involved. Something different, you know. And I owe it to Sybil not to look as though I've lost interest. She gave me my first break.'

'And mine too!'

'Yes, but I think it's dangerous mixing witchcraft with business. She's got a very successful studio. She's crazy to risk her reputation like this.'

'Is she?'

'Sybil uses girls who contact her studio for modelling work. Girls like yourself, trying to get into the business.'

'How do you mean, Peter? Uses them?'

'She channels suitable girls in the coven. Like she did you.'

'But what's wrong with that? I'm not complaining. I'm modelling as well.'

'It's procuring. Nothing less. Procuring girls for Gerald and his so-called followers. Under cover of witchcraft.'

'But it's white witchcraft, Peter. Not black and evil. Gerald said himself. Witchcraft can be a great power for good. And if a doctor believes in it, that's good enough for me.'

'What doctor?'

'Gerald. Doctor Amberley. He told Betty he was a doctor.'

'What's that got to do with it?'

'Well, he must know what's good for people's health.'

'Health? He's not that sort of doctor. He's not a doctor of medicine. He's a doctor of Literature. D.Litt. after his name. Nothing to do with medicine at all.'

'You're determined to try and put me off, aren't you? I don't really care what he is. It doesn't matter. He's a marvellous witch. And I don't mind playing along with Sybil either, so long as she makes me a top model. Cheap at any price, that's how I look at it.'

They stopped at the river bank, watching the water swirling by. Peter took her arm, turned her towards him, looked in her eyes. 'If you're that keen why not let me help you? You don't need her. With the right photographs I could make you famous myself.'

'But she's done it for other girls. Why shouldn't I let her do it for me? Anyway, you must be careful not to cross her. She's a very powerful woman. She might not like you taking my career over.'

'She doesn't exert a fraction of the power over me you do.'

Christine smiled. She loved the look in his eyes. 'I'm not talking about that sort of power, Peter.'

She kissed him where they stood and their mouths became tongue-locked again. They sank to the ground, without breaking the kiss. His hands reached for her greedily. As passion began to rise in them both, she responded, caressing him, stroking him - her hands exploring and exciting him with their soft touch. Suddenly he sat up, his face dark with anger.

'Peter! What's the matter.'

He took out a cigarette and lit it as he tried to phrase what he felt. He was not sure of himself. He couldn't understand what had happened and there was just a little fear mixed with the shame and impatience. How could he tell her? She propped herself on her elbow and looked at him searchingly. She was surprisingly calm and sympathetic.

'Peter, what is it?'

He was playing for time. Perhaps this moment would pass. 'Sybil. I don't think you really understand her.'

'Course I do. I know I haven't been in London long...'

'Why did you say that?...About Sybil?'

'Say what?' Christine was puzzled. She had no idea what was troubling him.

'That she had...a different power over me.'

'I think she really does have a witch's power. It wouldn't surprise me if she practised the Black Arts while still a member of Gerald's white coven.'

'I suppose that's what she was getting at when she warned me. Yesterday. If I ever touched you again she'd do more than fire me. But it's ridiculous! She can't really have supernatural powers. She just can't.' But his eyes belied the words.

'Well then, what are you worrying about?' She looked up at the sky, putting her arm round his neck, inviting him to lie down beside her again.

'Anyway, why should she threaten you? Just because you want me. You still do, don't you?'

He turned to lower his face to hers, holding his chest above her breasts with his hands as props on either side of her. 'Because she's jealous. And she wants you for herself. Can't you see?'

The significance of where she woke up that morning dawned on Christine. 'Stupid.'

'What?' Peter didn't follow her.

'No, me. I was just thinking how stupid I am. It all fits together.'

'I told her straight, Chris. You aren't like that.'

'I should hope not!'

'So she hasn't got that power either.'

'What power?'

'To get you. To attract you, sexually.'

'About the same chance she has of putting a spell on you.' Christine laughed, not realising she had evaded the question. 'Maybe I could put a spell on you? A stronger one.'

Peter lowered himself down onto her.

'I'll put one on you. One you'll like.' But a strange expression came over her face and she held herself stiff and tight-legged beneath him.

'No. We'd better get back.'

'Why?'

'She said something about taking more shots today. And if we're missing, we'll both be in trouble.'

'To hell with her!'

'Well, I'm not going to risk crossing her, even if you are.'

Christine slipped from under him and started to run for the house, laughing and skipping like a child. Peter looked after her in some annoyance. But he found it impossible to be angry with her.

'Catch you before you get there!' he called and began to make up the start she had already gained.

Johnny paused, beer tankard in hand. 'Pretty little place this, Wychwold. Never been here before.' He was trying to engage the landlord of the Witch's Broomstick in conversation. But Mine Host, untypically, was a man of few words. His philosophy was to pace out the day. He would have to make a lot of paid-for small talk before the final 'Time Gentlemen Please'. And as a member of the coven he had been well-schooled by Gerald in the art of answering strangers' questions cautiously without saying anything. He polished a glass and held it to the fairy lights round the low-ceilinged bar. 'Not bad. I like it.'

Johnny quaffed half his tankard in one swallow. 'Dearsay it attracts people?'

'Coach-loads at weekends.'

'Good for business?'

'Not bad.'

'I suppose they get to be a nuisance. Taking photos, that sort of thing?'

'You get used to it.' Another glass was polished.

'Fag?' Johnny offered his cigarette case.

'Don't use 'em, thanks.'

Johnny pocketed the case again. 'I suppose you get the professionals too, don't you? Photographers taking pictures for magazines.'

'Sometimes.'

'Do they mostly come after the views? Cottages and trees, that sort? Or do you get the other type, fashion stuff? Girls against country backgrounds. For instance, outside your place here. They use all sorts of places these days.'

'Do they?'

'You don't happen to have seen one I'm trying to contact? Quite well-known in London. Sybil Waite?'

''Scuse me a moment - I must have a word with the girl in the snug.' The landlord went through to the other bar to speak to the barmaid. Johnny took another pull on his bitter, and tried again as he returned.

'You don't know her then? She's supposed to have been down here for the weekend.'

'What name?'

C
H
A
P
T
E
R

T
W
E
L
V
E

107

'Sybil Waite.' He can't be that dumb, thought Johnny.

'Not that I know of. We get customers from all over. Come down from London or wherever and I get chatting to them without knowing who they are, if you follow my meaning. Sometimes for years I've known 'em. They come in odd times.'

'She may have had a couple of young girls with her. Very professional career woman, she is. Big wheel in the advertising world. Thought she might have been in here, that's all.' Johnny tried to keep it off-hand.

'Sorry. Can't help you.'

Johnny drank up and pushed the tankard across the counter as he turned for the door.

'Good day sir.' The landlord smiled thoughtfully as the door closed behind Johnny. Then he moved to the telephone.

Christine knocked at Sybil's bedroom but did not wait for an invitation to enter. Did she see Sybil put her hands quickly behind her, as if hiding something she didn't want Christine to see? It was a guilty sort of movement even though she greeted Christine with a welcoming smile.

'Christina, dear! I thought you'd gone out.' Sybil turned to the window, bringing one hand round the blind-side of her body and secreting whatever was in it behind the curtain on the pretence of looking out of the window.

Christine knew then she was not mistaken. She laughed to cover her curiosity. 'I ran up to the top of the hill and back. It's put me in good shape for any work you want today.'

'Oh, I see. Splendid.'

The balance of power seemed to be shifting. Christine was using the attraction she now strongly suspected she had. An emotional see-saw. Sybil's dominance began to decrease as Christine asserted herself.

'I didn't wake you, did I, Sybil? When I slipped out of bed this morning? You were sleeping so peacefully, it seemed a shame to.'

'No. No. I er...I wondered where you were, of course, when I opened my eyes.'

Sybil appeared to be embarrassed. Christine confidently strolled around the room as if quite unconcerned about anything. She reached the window, the one where Sybil had hidden whatever it was she was holding.

Christine looked out with the same pretence as Sybil had used. 'You can see the Witches' Ring from here, can't you? Poor Peter! He seemed very down and dopey. Too many late nights.' She was about to move the curtain when Sybil took her arm and drew her away from the window. Sybil was anxious.

'Did he...Did he bother you at all? You know what I mean?'

'Bother me? You mean make a pass? Yes, he did. But I'm quite able to take care of myself. I can handle Peter, and anything he tries to start.'

If Peter had heard her say this he would have died, she smiled to herself secretly.

Sybil did not try to hide her relief. 'I'm glad of that. Because he doesn't seem to take any notice of my warning.'

'Don't worry on my account, Sybil. It'd bother me much more if men didn't make passes at me. Anyway, he's so young. And not the strong silent type, let's face it.'

'You prefer someone older?'

'Well, let's say not my own age, anyway.' Sybil smiled unaware that Christine was playing with her.

'You'll always have to watch the photo boys, darling. Even when you're at the top. They think it's one of their perks.'

'To have it off with their models? They'll find I don't treat anyone as God Almighty. Certainly not photographers.' She looked straight at Sybil to make sure she got the comparison. 'My career is entirely in your hands.'

Sybil took her arms and drew her close. 'Then you're going a long way. Christina. I promise you.'

'I hope so. I shall dedicate myself to whatever you want me to do.'

'If we work as closely as that - as close as we are now - you need have no doubts at all. You will go to the top.'

'If I'm half as successful as you are, I'll be happy. May I ask you one question? It's a bit personal?'

'I don't mind how personal. I'll keep nothing from you. And I expect the same in return.'

'Has it helped you? Being a witch?'

Sybil paused a moment and then laughed.

'The whole advertising business is witchcraft, darling. We have to keep the poor old public spellbound. And we do.'

'I hadn't thought of it that way.'

'And now we're in partnership, they'd better watch out. We make a formidable pair, you know that.'

Sybil drew her so close their bodies were touching. Christine's eyes stayed cold, even though she was trying to soften them. But Sybil was so intent that she didn't notice. She kissed Christine, who tried not to compare the feel of her lips with Peter's or Gerald's. She had been wondering how she would feel when Sybil began to make her intentions as overt as this; whether she'd be able to take it without showing her distaste. To her surprise she didn't feel anything. No emotion at all.

Christine purposely stepped back to break off the kiss before Sybil was ready, then she turned to face the window calculating her move precisely. She had not forgotten that hidden behind the curtain was something Sybil did not want her to see.

Sybil played right into her hands. 'You don't mind? My kissing you? I like to show my affection.'

Christine turned as if thinking of her answer, away from Sybil, still close to the window. 'No, no. I don't think so. It's just...it's never happened before.'

Maybe when she was a top model Christine would try her hand at acting; she was finding it very easy to be convincing.

Sybil came close behind her, put her hands on her shoulders and whispered in her ear. 'I don't want to rush you, darling. But I'm glad I'm the first. The first woman to tell you that she loves you.'

Christine took one more step and was at the window. 'I need to get used to the idea, Sybil, that's all. You do understand?'

'I understand. Completely. I remember when it first happened to me.'

Christine's hand had crept behind the curtain. She pulled out a wax doll, secreted by Sybil on the windowledge. Christine pretended she didn't know what it was even though the pins sticking in its head and body made it quite obvious.

'What's this? Some sort of doll?'

Sybil held out her hand for it but Christine pretended not to notice. 'Were you putting a spell on someone, Sybil?'

'Oh, it isn't that important.' Her hand stayed out.

'But it is, darling. If someone's done you harm, you must tell me. And tell me how you can get your own back...with this.'

'It doesn't matter. It really doesn't. I thought that - Anyway, I was wrong. That's why it doesn't matter.'

'Could it have been...Peter?'

Sybil was completely in her hands. She nodded, submissively.

Christine laughed. 'Well, you mustn't put a spell on him now. Or if you have, you must take it off. It might affect his work. That wouldn't do me any good, would it?'

Christine held out the model, but when Sybil tried to take it, she withdrew a little.

'Take the pins out first.'

Sybil did exactly as she was told, while Christine kept a tight hold on the doll.

'Last one, Sybil. Now. The doll itself. In the basket.'

Christine handed her the doll and had a marvellous feeling of power as Sybil obediently took it to the leather-covered drum and dropped it in.

'There! I told you it didn't mater,' observed Sybil, trying to justify her acquiescence.

'You can trust me to do whatever is necessary with Peter. Leave him entirely to me.'

'I will. I'm quite happy now.' Sybil's voice was unusually mild.

Christine smiled her winning-over smile and walked out with a sense of achievement. She had done something worth doing. It was a feeling she'd never had in her life before.

The milkman was on the last leg of his daily round when Johnny pulled up the Jaguar beside him. 'Know anywhere round here they're taking pictures?'

'Pictures?' The milkman stacked the empties on his float and took three pints off.

'Have you seen a fashion photographer working anywhere round here?'

The milkman shook his head dumbly. He turned away and negotiated the rickety gate of a thatched cottage. 'Nearest place I know is a shop in the town. High Street, I think.

Passports and weddings. That what you want?' And he disappeared round the side of the cottage to the back door.

Johnny pulled a face. 'Thanks for nothing.' And he drove off.

Lucifer was curled up on Gerald's desk, seemingly with one half-opened eye on what he was writing. The cat turned its head lazily as Christine's voice came from the open French doors, which led from the book-lined study to the terrace.

'Am I disturbing you?'

Gerald rose to meet her as she entered. 'Not at all, my dear. In fact -' he indicated the coffee table where Wendell, who had carried in the girls' cases when they arrived, was putting down a tray. 'I was expecting you. See? I ordered coffee for two, didn't I, Wendell?'

'You did, sir,' came the solemn reply.

'You must be psychic.'

Gerald smiled. 'Yes.' And they laughed, sharing the joke. 'Will you pour?'

'Of course.' As Wendell left, Christine sat and picked up the beautiful antique silver coffee jug. 'I've got a few minutes break while Sybil and Peter work out a new set-up. So I thought I would use it to...come and say thank you.'

Gerald took her hand as she set down his coffee cup. He kissed her palm like an Eighteenth Century gallant might have done. 'Dear Christina. It was meant to be.'

Somehow she didn't find the gesture overdone. 'I feel it was, too. Over the last few days, I've had to do certain things. As if I was compelled to, forced to almost. And they were all leading me here. To Wychwold.'

'Do you realise, child, you have great gifts? You possess marvellous power. You must always use it as well as you possibly can.'

'I hope you will teach me how.'

'I will. Everything I know myself.'

He went over to the book-lined wall, straight to a particular shelf to pick out a special volume.

'Read this book of mine for a start. That is the right grounding for you.'

'You have got a lot of books. It's like having your own

library.'

'It is a library. A library of witchcraft. Every known book on the subject is there. But that one is by me.'

'You wrote it! Oh yes - by Gerald Amberley. You must have been studying for years and years.'

'Not quite that long. You make me sound as if I'm in my dotage. I first got interested at University. But yes. you're right, it is a few years ago now. There are so many theories. It takes time. My life's study.'

Christine was looking along the shelves when her eye rested on another book. She picked it out, Gerald's own book tucked under her arm. 'Oooh, spells! Bet that's fascinating.'

Gerald pointedly took the book from her and put it back. 'Spells mean Black Magic, Christina. That is something you must never meddle in. Never!' His voice and expression were stern.

'But there is something to it?'

'Undoubtedly. That's why it's much too risky to tinker with.'

'Does Sybil get her spells from books like that?'

Gerald alerted. 'Sybil? Is Sybil casting spells?'

'I'm not sure. I believe she tried to put one on Peter.'

'Why Peter, for heaven's sake?'

Christine shrugged. 'I know he's very down. He thinks it's because of a spell. Course, he could have imagined it.'

Gerald was concerned, but tried to seem off-hand about the idea. 'I expect that's it. It's easy to imagine all sorts of things.'

'Gerald. Could I become a High Priestess?'

'Certainly. When you initiate another.'

'I'd like that.'

'I see no reason why you shouldn't go even further. Form a coven of your own one day. Find your own High Priest.'

Christine gave a little yelp of pleasure. Her coffee cup rattled on its saucer with her excitement.

'I mean it, Christina! You are capable of reaching that elevated state. If you desire it enough.' Then he continued quite casually as if reverting to small-talk. 'How about your sister? Does the supernatural interest her? Would she like to join us? If you invited her?'

'Betty? She'd be scared stiff!'

Gerald raised his eyebrows. 'That would make it all the

more pleasurable, surely. I feel we could do so much for her. Bring her out of herself.'

'I'm sure we could. I agree with you there.'

'Well then...why don't we?' Gerald let Christine make the running.

'We'd have to take it gently. Suggest it at the right time. Talk her round gradually.'

'You have sufficient influence over her. You are twins, after all. You are the dominant one. And now...You are a witch. Test your powers. You'll be agreeably surprised.'

'Yes, I must. If I get her to agree - could I initiate her myself?'

Gerald was thoughtful. He stared out of the windows. 'Mmmmm. Of course Sybil is the High Priestess of my coven...at the moment.'

Christine secretly registered the importance of those last three words. She followed his gaze.

In the garden Sybil was discussing shots and angles with Peter. She stopped and felt her ear, just as if it had suddenly started burning. Christine and Gerald exchanged smiles.

Colonel Cruickshank was walking his Great Dane along the lane leading out of the village when Johnny pulled up and asked him the routine questions. The Colonel didn't even let him get started.

'Look here, young man. I don't know who you are or where you come from but we don't like strangers around here. We're a quiet little spot in the backwaters, and we don't want it disturbed by interlopers who can't even speak the Queen's English.'

And to Johnny's jaw-dropping surprise he stuck his chin out and marched off in a huff. It was all too quick even for one of Johnny's sharp comebacks.

Johnny drove on to try his luck yet again. Further down the lane, he had to jam on his brakes as two girls leaped out of his way, laughing their apologies. Johnny did not move off again immediately. He frowned with concentration, trying to remember. Just where had he seen those two birds before? He lit himself a cigarette, all the time watching them in his rear-view mirror. He saw them stop to chat to the Colonel type, who raised his hat to them politely. One of the girls struck a stance that gave Johnny the answer in a flash. They were the two girls who had modelled for the nude mural in Sybil Waite's studio. He was sure. Well, as good as sure, that was near enough for him

He was about to back up and ask them about Sybil when the Colonel noticed the parked Jaguar and pointed to it with his walking stick. Johnny thought again, and drove slowly on, looking at the larger houses in their own grounds, which now flanked the lane.

'That's better.' Christine had come from the terrace to find Betty playing with Lucifer on the lawn.

'What?'

'There's a smile on your face, for a change!'

She took Betty's arm and they walked off down the path to the Florentine fountain.

'I'd feel even better if I could be sure I'd hear from Johnny this morning.'

'Stop worrying! Either you will or you won't. Worrying won't alter it.'

'I suppose not. But if I never see him again, what about that packet I'm keeping for him?'

Christine still decided not to tell her the story behind that. She shrugged. 'That's his worry. Have to come and get it, won't he? But I won't think much of him if that's all he comes for.'

Betty looked so miserable that Christine gave her an affectionate hug and laughed it off.

'Cheer up! I promised you everything would go right, didn't I?'

'Sorry, Chris. I wish I could be as sure of things as you are.'

'Just think how well things have gone since we left home. We're really on our way, Betty. Believe me!'

'Well, you are. You'll be famous. I'd like to see their faces back home when they see your picture in the papers. On a front cover, perhaps. Think of that, Chris!'

'You know the first thing we do when we get back to London?'

'No. What?'

'Look for a flat and move out of that crummy old room.'

'It's better than nothing. We ought to be grateful for it.'

'We are! But we don't have to be any longer!'

'Can we afford something better?'

'On the money Sybil says I'll be earning - easily.'

'I can't believe it's real, I can't, honestly! It's all happened so quickly.'

'You'd better start getting used to it. Because it isn't a dream.'

'It's all your doing, Chris. I'd never have had the nerve by myself.'

'We're going to change that. Very soon.'

'How d'you mean? Change me?'

'No, not change you. Your personality.'

'How?'

'I'll explain later. Just for now, promise me one thing.'

'What's that?'

'Promise me you'll stay here tonight. Even if Johnny wants you to go back. If he comes you can be with him all day. He can monopolise you every minute if he likes. But I want you to stay tonight. That's not too much to ask, is it?'

'Of course not.'

'Promise?'

'I promise. But why -' Betty stopped as she saw Johnny's Jaguar going slowly past the open gates. 'Johnny! That's his car. I'm sure of it!'

Betty made a dash for the gates. Christine smiled. Now Betty had promised, it didn't matter whether it was Johnny's car or not. Not to Christine.

Johnny had seen them too and backed up. As he turned into the drive he opened the door and Betty got in, making no secret of her delight in seeing him. She kissed him, oblivious of the fact that he had to keep within the verges of the drive, if he was not to be an unwelcome guest.

Christine paused at the French doors to the study and shook her head at Betty's effusive welcome. Then she became serious and looked in to see if the room was empty. After a quick glance around, she slid inside quietly.

She went straight to the shelf where the book on spells was kept. She leafed through it, looking for something - something special...

CHAPTER THIRTEEN

In the way of young people in love, it had not taken Betty and Johnny long to discover the privacy of the river bank. They were wrapped in each other's arms, totally unaware of the natural beauties around them.

'You've no idea what I've been through trying to find you!' Johnny told her, the words muffled as he nuzzled against her neck. 'No one in this god-forsaken place wanted to know. One character said I didn't even talk proper English. It's like a foreign country down here. You had me dead worried, I'll tell you.'

Betty laughed. She was so happy. The more trouble he'd been through, the more it proved he wanted to see her.

'What's so funny about that, then?'

'Nothing. It's nice to know you worried about me.'

'Course I did, stupid!' This was so lovingly said that she had to kiss him. He responded, almost pinning her to the ground.

'You know, Baby, you're not safe to be allowed out alone.'

His concern gave her a thrill deep inside, but she pretended to be offended. He was treating her like a child. 'Do you mind? We're doing nicely, thank you very much, without your help. Everything's going like a bomb. Life's wonderful! Even better now.'

Johnny hoped she meant what her eyes told him. 'Now?'

The confirmation was whispered and warm. 'Yes, now. Now you're here, Johnny.'

Johnny held her tight. He kissed her neck, her ear, her trembling lips. And then murmured: 'If anyone hurt you, I reckon I'd kill 'em.'

'Why should anyone hurt me?'

'They'd better not! I'm just trying to explain how I feel that's all. I don't know what's got into me. Going all soft over a bird. I never have before.'

'Is that the absolute truth?'

'I wouldn't lie to you, Betty. I've had lots of girls in my time. But I've never felt like I do right now.'

'Are you saying...you love me?'

'Love' was the one word Johnny had been skating all round. He felt embarrassed - shy even. Shy - him? He was in a state!

'Do you, Johnny?'

'Well, you know, it's silly innit, this love bit?'

'Not if you mean it. If I can say it, you can!'

'You haven't! You haven't said it.'

'Well, I do.'

'That's not saying it.'

Betty looked him straight in the eyes. 'I...love...you.'

'Certain?' Johnny couldn't believe his good fortune. He suddenly felt like a giant. Confident of tackling anything in the world.

'I'll never be like this about anyone else. I couldn't. It must be love, Johnny, mustn't it?'

'Suppose so. First time for me, too. There you are, I've said it. I love you.'

They kissed. A long, loving, intimate promise. Johnny helped Betty to her feet. 'Right then. Let's celebrate.' He took Betty's hands and began to lead her back towards the house.

'Celebrate? How? There's nowhere to go round here!'

'Back in town, there is.'

'Now? You mean right away?'

'Nothing to keep us here, is there?'

'No. Except...'

Johnny looked at her with a frown. She smiled apologetically. 'Chris wants me to stay. Until tomorrow.'

'What for? Something special?'

'Don't think so. She just asked me to promise I would. So I did.' She cuddled her arm through his. 'Doesn't matter though. We've got all day together, haven't we?'

'I'd rather get away from here.'

'Why? It's a lovely place.'

'I dunno. There's something about the natives round these parts. Makes the hair stand up on my neck. You know the feeling?'

'You haven't even met them yet.'

'I've met enough of 'em in the village. Right old lot! And I know enough about Sybil Waite not to want to meet her, thank you.'

Betty withdrew her arm. 'What d'you mean by that?'

'She's got a reputation.'

'Of course! That's success for you.'

'Not her professional reputation. Friend of mine pulled a very funny face when I mentioned her. She's supposed to fancy young girls.'

Betty looked at him to see if he was really serious. He was. 'You wouldn't kid me?'

'Don't imagine there aren't women like that. As randy as dirty old men. Worse, some of 'em.'

'Well, don't worry. She hasn't shown the slightest interest in me.'

'All the more reason to get going before she does.'

'Don't be silly! It's Chris she's -' Betty stopped dead in her tracks. 'So that's it! That's why Chris is so keen for me to stay with her tonight.'

'She made you promise that?'

'Well, that was how she put it. I can't remember her exact words. But I did promise.'

'You don't have to play nanny to Christine, surely? She can look after herself, if anyone can. Particularly against another female, I'd've thought.'

'If she wants me to stay, Johnny, that's it. She might need me. Don't let's row about it.'

Johnny was getting angry. 'Who's having a row?'

She looked at his thunderous face and couldn't resist a smile. This only made him angrier.

'All I'm asking is that you come back with me. Now. But if I don't mean that much to you and you'd rather stay -'

Betty was indignant. 'It's not that. I told you.'

'Look, she's a big girl now. She can look after herself. You know that as well as I do.'

'That's not the point. It's obvious why she wants me to stay - because of...what you say about Sybil Waite. I might be able to help. It's important. She's working, you know. It's not just a weekend off for Chris.'

'I'm not bothered about her. It's you I don't like getting mixed up in it.'

'I'm not mixed up in anything.'

His face was grim and he turned away from Betty impatiently. 'I don't like it, I tell you.'

She stood her ground, trying not to show that she was frightened - not only of Johnny's anger but that she might have been damaging their now-found relationship too. 'Since we're on the subject, there are one or two things I don't like either!' she said defiantly.

'What's that supposed to mean?'

'What about Abby Drake?'

'Well, what about her?'

'Giving you fancy presents. Is she just a client? Or is there more to it than that?'

Johnny kicked at a tuft of grass. 'Not any more. If you must know.'

'So there was?'

'Yes. Was. It's over. Satisfied?'

'How do I know that?'

''Cos I'm telling you. And I don't tell lies. It was over before I met you. Look, if it worries you I'll tell her to get someone else to look after her cars then I won't have to see her again. I can get by without her business. It is strictly business these days, that's all.'

Betty smiled. 'You'd do that, if I wanted you to?'

'Course. She means nothing to me, I tell you.'

'Oh, Johnny!' She kissed him. He took her hand, trying once more to lead her towards the parked Jaguar.

'Come on, then.'

She pulled her hand free and shook her head.

'Look, d'you want to stick to Christine like Siamese twins? Or are you coming with me? Simple as that?'

'Please don't ask me to choose now, Johnny. I promised.'

Johnny made for the Jag. 'Okay then...'

'Johnny!' Betty pleaded urgently.

Johnny stopped and turned. 'Coming?'

'I...no, I can't.'

Johnny's face darkened. 'That's it, then, isn't it?'

He turned and stormed off. If he had seen the tears welling into her eyes, he would have come running back to her immediately. But he didn't. He got into the car, slammed the door and drove off. The wheels spat out gravel as if reflecting his fury.

Gerald had been watching the scene from a distance. Now he put on his Number One smile and approached the hunched up picture of misery. She looked up as he said: 'And what are you doing with yourself today, dear?' By this time Johnny was out of her sight, though not her mind.

The dining room table had been laid in all its Amberley glory. The candles were lit, although the preparations were not for a real meal. Christine was posed, cider bottle in hand, as if about to fill a long-stemmed glass. Sybil watched as Peter clicked for yet another shot.

'This should be the last.' Click. 'Fine. Super, Christine.'

Sybil clapped her hands twice in token pleasure. 'I've never known anyone pick up the tricks so fast. Well done, my dear.'

Peter was already packing his lights. 'I'd better mark these up before I forget the sequence. It's been a pretty complex session.'

'Should have a good set of pix there, Peter.' Sybil never allowed her animosity to enter their professional partnership.

'Should have - thanks to our new model. Won't be long.'

Peter collected his equipment and shut the door behind him. Sybil put her hand on Christine's upper arm and caressed it sensuously. Christine steeled herself to smile, disguising her inner feelings.

'How do you feel? Now you've done your first job?' Her hands rested lightly on Christine's hips.

'It's great.'

'I'm very proud of you, my lovely.'

Without warning, she pulled Christine to her, and Christine found herself in a tight embrace before she could avoid it. Sybil's kiss had to be suffered. To turn her cheek at this stage would have seemed like a definite rebuff. As soon as she dared, Christine pushed gently to indicate she wanted to break free.

'Christina! What's the matter, darling?'

'Someone might come in. Peter said he wouldn't be long.'

It sounded lame to Sybil, who was eyeing her suspiciously, but not letting her go.

'Please Sybil. If someone did...'

Sybil asked quite deliberately: 'Tonight?'

Christine took her time. She knew she was walking a tightrope but so far she'd managed to keep her balance. 'Maybe...if it's possible...' She was thinking of the plan she'd been making.

'It will be. After the ceremony. Gerald wants to hold another Sabbat tonight.'

'Yes, he did tell me.' But Christine was completely unprepared for the next piece of information.

'He'd like me to initiate Betty.'

Christine stiffened. She fought her emotions. This was no time to give anything away.

'Did he say that?' She appeared quite cool even under Sybil's shrewd and penetrating scrutiny.

'You've no objection, have you, Christina?'

'I'm not objecting. I'm just thinking of Betty. She's not said she's keen... And you know I was.' She simply could not admit that she knew Betty would die at the thought of Sybil initiating her.

'You could easily put her mind at rest. I haven't the slightest doubt that you could persuade her...if you wanted to.'

'I wouldn't. Not against her will.'

'Then leave it up to her.'

'No! You're not having Betty in your coven. Not yet. Not until I say she's ready.'

Sybil's voice took on a threatening, almost menacing note. 'I don't think you quite understand the position. Once you are a member of a coven, you are bound to it. You must abide by the rules. The first rule, Christina, is obedience. To your High Priest - Gerald. And to your High Priestess - me!'

Christine had no answer.

Sybil's eyes were hard. 'Betty will be initiated tonight.'

Christine stared back in silence. Then she walked past Sybil and left the dining room. Peter met her just outside the open door as she swept out.

Peter appealed to Sybil: 'Where's she off to?' He turned to see Christine disappearing into the garden. 'Chris! Wait for me!'

Sybil strode to the door and stared venomously after them both. If looks could kill...

Christine had gone off with such fury that Peter didn't catch up with her until she was approaching the path through the woods.

'Chris! Didn't you hear me shouting? What's the big hurry?'

'I just want to walk, that's all.'

'Okay, I don't mind.'

Christine stopped. 'Alone. I want time to think.'

Peter noticed her stormy expression. He could hardly not do so. 'What's up, Chris? Something Sybil said?'

She didn't answer. The thought of it darkened her face even more.

'You've had a row! You were all right when I took my stuff out of the dining room. The old bitch made a pass at you? I bet that's it!'

'I don't want to talk about it.'

Peter took her arm with concern. 'But I do.'

'Let me go, Peter. Please.' She shook free of him and walked on. Peter realised she meant it. That she didn't want any help or advice from him. He stood watching her disappear into the trees. And wished that just once he could make some-one do what he wanted them to do. Particularly someone like Christine.

As Christine walked, she began to move stealthily, swaying between the trees, picking her path carefully, like a young cat. It was an involuntary change. She only became aware of it after it happened.

For no apparent reason, she stopped absolutely dead and did not move a muscle. Only wisps of hair trembled in the breeze. Her lips tightened and her eyes began to gleam with venom not unlike the look Sybil threw after her only a moment ago.

Then she nodded slowly to herself, as if realisation had come to her of what she must do. She bent down and collected dry twigs from around the roots of trees. She began to form them into a pattern on the ground.

When it was complete the twigs spelt out 'SYBIL'. Christine took two more twigs and rubbed them together angrily. She had never done that before, but had no doubt of her capability to make it work. Her anger spurred her efforts and soon a wisp of smoke was turned to fire.

She applied the burning twigs to the pattern on the ground. It kindled quickly. Christine's eyes glowed as the name burned brightly. For a moment 'Sybil' was written in glowing fire. Then it slowly disappeared into wood-ash.

She scraped the white powder together with her hands.

Strangely it did not burn her. She didn't even feel the heat in her impatience. It was beginning to cool by the time she had scooped it into her handkerchief.

She straightened up and listened. All she could hear was the gentle burbling of water moving down the river. She smiled, drawn by the direction of the sound.

At the river's edge, she threw out her handkerchief, holding onto one corner. The ashes scattered onto the surface of the river. Christine watched them float away and gradually disappear in the surface-bubbling. She stood motionless as the anger in her face subsided, to be replaced by a sardonic smile - a smile never seen on Christine's face before.

Sybil gave a sharp cry and dropped her glass. Sherry spilled over the mahogany coffee table. Gerald put his own drink down and moved quickly to her.

'My dear, what is it?'

Sybil was patently in severe pain. She pressed both hands to her head, her face was white and strained. 'I...I don't know. Sorry, Gerald. I suddenly...felt this terrible pain. Like a...red hot knife boring through my head.'

Gerald surveyed her sympathetically, but was equally concerned for his Pembroke table. He mopped up the wine with his handkerchief.

'I'll get you another drink.'

'No. Please. Thank you, Gerald. I don't want anything.'

Peter came in. Seeing Sybil in some distress, he raised his eyebrows enquiringly at Gerald. He went to the cabinet to pour himself a drink, asking: 'Not too good, Sybil?' His voice conveyed little concern.

Gerald frowned at him. 'She got a sudden pain, that's all. Still there?'

'Yes. Not quite so bad though.'

Peter brought his glass and joined them. 'Must be something going around. I felt a bit rough myself first thing. Right as rain now. Can't understand it.' He looked hard at Sybil, as she passed her hand slowly across her brow.

'It's coming back again. I think I'll lie down for a while.'

They helped her to stand. 'Shall I cancel tonight?' Gerald

suggested.

'No. No, don't do that. I'll be all right after a rest. It will pass. I'm sure.'

They watched her go, Gerald genuinely concerned, Peter fighting to hide a grin of satisfaction.

Sybil entered her bedroom with her hands still pressed to her temples. She went to the windows to shut out the daylight, screwing her eyes tight with the unbearable pain.

Drawing the curtains did not put the room in complete darkness, but the dim light was some relief. She moved slowly to the bed and drew back the covers. She stepped back with a gasp of horror. A black toad sat on the top sheet, hunched ready to jump, its throat pulsing as if pumping it up larger and larger.

Sybil was gasping with shock. The pain shot through her head.

'Gerald's just told me you're not feeling well.'

The calm voice came from the doorway. She turned to see Christine framed there.

'I'm all right, thank you.' Sybil was suspicious. The girl's face expressed sympathy, but her arrival was rather too much of a coincidence.

Christine noticed the toad. 'How on earth did that get here?'

Sybil was sure she knew. 'Someone must have put it there,' she replied coldly. She was beginning to suspect Christine but the thought was too frightening. She dared not face it. And yet the pain in her head - that revolting toad. She felt sick.

Christine had no such qualms. She picked up the harmless creature and took it to the window. She drew back one curtain, making Sybil flinch at the light. She opened the window and put the toad on the sill outside. 'There you are, feller. It's a long jump down, so be careful.' She closed the window and curtain again.

'You going to bed then? Anything I can get you?'

'No... No thank you.' Sybil spoke with undertones of fear.

Christine was matter of fact. 'So sorry I rushed off like that. It's not me that's upsetting you, I hope?'

Sybil would have liked to accuse her straight out, but thought better of it. She shook her head.

'I didn't mean to.' She gripped Sybil's arm, tightly. 'You do look rotten. You must lie down for a bit. That's what you need.' It was a gentle order. Her hand directed Sybil towards the bed.

'I'm all right, I tell you. The pain's beginning to go.'

'You're worrying about tonight, aren't you? Being all right for the ceremony. Why don't you let me help? Just tell me what do to.'

Sybil couldn't tell whether Christine was forcing her to lie down, or helping her. The only way she could try to exert any dominance was to say, through the pain: 'I'm the High Priestess.'

'Of course you are. I know that. It's only for tonight...' Christine's hand pressed Sybil's shoulders back until she was lying prostrate on her back. 'There's no point in cracking up, just for the sake of one Sabbat.'

'Christine, why are you fighting me?'

Christine smiled as if comforting a small child. She lifted her hands from Sybil's shoulders and placed her feet together, as if nursing her. 'That's ridiculous. Why should I fight you? After all I have to thank you for? All you've done for me?'

Sybil touched Christine's arm, a pitiful gesture. 'Don't do it! Don't! Please!'

Christine assumed a plausible expression of bewilderment. 'I'm not doing anything, Sybil. It was only a suggestion. If you're all right in time for the ceremony, the question doesn't arise at all. I only want to help.'

Sybil raised her head. The pain seared through and she pressed her fingers to her temples again. 'I shall be at the ceremony. I must be!'

Christine flashed the big smile that always won Betty over. 'See you there then.' And she left the bedroom.

The line-up of empty tankards - even though they were only halves - was a measure of how much Johnny was trying to drown his sorrow. But he was far from being 'stoned' and instantly recognised the twit who thought he didn't speak the same language when the Colonel entered the Saloon door and joined the attractive horsewoman at the bar. Johnny downed the dregs of his current half and went over to re-order. It was a premeditated move to eavesdrop.

'My usual please, old boy,' ordered the Colonel, and turned to engage his companion in conversation. They talked quietly but Johnny's left ear locked on like a radar dish as he watched the landlord drain a whisky optic twice for the Colonel's 'usual'.

If Johnny didn't speak the same language, he'd show this twit they drank the same poison. 'Double scotch, please.' He intended his words to be overheard.

'Just a minute, I'm serving.' The landlord still hadn't accepted Johnny as a welcome customer in spite of the money he'd already added to the day's takings.

The Colonel took his whisky from the counter without turning his attention from his horsey companion. Johnny strained to make the sotto voce syllables intelligible. 'You know old Gerald's laying on another one tonight?' the Colonel whispered.

'Yes. I got the message along the grapevine.'

'Doing us proud, what? Isn't he?'

'Hope it doesn't mean he's putting up the subscription. It's steep enough as -'

'Now sir, your double whisky.' The landlord caused Johnny to miss a vital snatch. 'You got the right money, I'm short of change.' Johnny got it over with, sipped his whisky and picked up the conversation again.

The woman was speaking even more quietly and Johnny had to lean in their direction to catch anything. 'Any idea what the new girl's like?'

'Pretty little thing. I've seen her.' The Colonel fingered his moustache with relish. Johnny only just restrained himself from physical violence. But if he broke up the conversation now he might miss some vital snippet of information.

'Young and innocent, I hope.' the woman's lips curled

sadistically. 'The last one took it far too eagerly for my tastes. I like a bit of resistance, bags of fear. Much better stuff.'

'But she was a beauty.' The Colonel talked as if he had been inspecting the troops. 'The new one should suit you better though. Looks a bit naive. You know, red raw recruit type.'

The woman nodded. 'Like this mare I'm breaking in. All the more satisfying when you finally bend them to your will.'

Johnny gulped his whisky down. Was it possible they were talking about Betty? Both sisters could be described as new girls but no one would call Christine naive. He knocked back the dregs of his glass. The neat spirit was already beginning to take effect, but he knew that he mustn't get involved in a punch-up at this stage. Keep your head clear, Johnny boy. Think things out. What to do? Perhaps fresh air would help. He fixed his eyes on the door and walked a somewhat unsteady line towards it.

Betty lay on the bed, red-eyed from crying. Christine was sitting at her side, holding her hand tightly.

'Betty, you can't go on like this! It isn't doing any good.'

Betty sobbed, but had no tears left. 'I shan't see him again. I know I shan't. Ever.'

'Don't be silly. Of course you will.'

'How do you know? You weren't there. He was fed up with me. Went off in a huff. He'll find someone who won't treat him like I did.'

'Oh, do shut up!' Her sharp tone made Betty stop and look up at her. Christine lectured her.

'How many more times do I have to say it before you'll believe me? You don't have any faith in what I can do, that's your trouble. Just because we're sisters and you've known me since we were little, you think I can't do things you can't do. Have I ever promised anything that hasn't come true?'

'Well, no...but -'

'What?' Christine pressed her again.

'Johnny said I had to choose between him and you.'

'What a load of rubbish! Choose between us. Whatever for? Can't you have a sister and a boyfriend? If he really loves you, he'd put up with me if I were the worst sister in the world.'

'You're not. You're the best!'

'Then what's he on about? It's a good test. If he loves you, he'll be back.'

'He does love me! He said he did just now...oh, I don't know what to think.'

'We'll find out. You've got to see him again, anyway.'

'Why have I got to...?'

'If he wants that package he left.'

'Oh, yes, I'd forgotten about that.'

'You can bet your life he hasn't!'

'How do you know?'

'It's too important for him to forget.'

Betty looked at her enquiringly. 'Why do you say that?'

'You haven't learned much about the boy you've fallen for, have you? I warned you at the start, he's a sharp character.'

'That's not fair! What's he done to you to deserve it? He's been very sweet and kind. Until...I wouldn't go with him.'

Christine had gone to her bedside-table and taken something from the drawer. Now she swung round to hold it up dramatically. It was the small white package.

'Chris! That's Johnny's. You took it from my case!'

'And you know what's inside it?'

'It's nothing to do with us.'

'If it's in our possession, it certainly is. You can be had up for carrying drugs.'

'Drugs!' Betty was incredulous, her eyes widening in horror. 'Are you sure?'

'D'you think I'd say that if I wasn't? Peddling drugs, that's what your Mister Johnny "Pusher" Dixon is up to. And he could be in big trouble giving it to you. You're still a minor in law. If the police found out, he'd really be for it.'

'I...I don't believe it. I just can't...not of Johnny.'

'You trust him more than you trust me, then. Thanks.'

'Chris, you're not going to tell the police - please!'

'You still feel the same about him? Now you know about this?'

Betty was totally confused. Only a few moments ago she had felt she couldn't live without him, her perfect man, everything she wanted in life. 'I can't believe it. Not Johnny.' She kept on repeating this, as if to convince herself.

'Well, here's the evidence. You're not seeing things. Want to try it?'

'No! No! But I don't believe Johnny would be mixed up in anything like that. He's not bad, I know he isn't. There must be some explanation.'

'Sure, he'll have an explanation if you ask him. That's for certain. But you can bet it's one the police will have heard a million times before.'

Betty got up from the bed and grabbed Christine by the arm. 'Please don't tell them. Let me find out first...from Johnny. Please don't get him into trouble, Chris. Please! For my sake.'

'So you still go for him all the way? In spite of this?'

'I don't want him to get into trouble because of me. Don't let that happen.'

Christine was playing her cards in a planned sequence. 'It doesn't have to happen. I could even get him back for you, if you want.'

Betty looked amazed. 'How?'

'See? You still haven't faith in what I can do.'

'I have, Chris! But how? I don't see how?'

Betty's defences were down. 'Crazy. Absolutely crazy. If you told me he was a murderer, I don't believe it would make any difference. I just wouldn't believe it, that's all. I'd love him whatever I found out about him.'

'You'd help me get him back for you?'

'I'd do anything! Yes.'

'Become a witch?'

Betty gasped. Her mind raced back, recollecting the unexplained events since they arrived. 'The chapel. That's where you were, when you said you'd been downstairs for a drink? They've made you one!'

Christine smiled her winning smile. 'It's wonderful, Betty!' But for the first time in their lives, the smile didn't work instantly.

'I couldn't...' Betty's face showed fear, not revulsion.

Christine turned and walked to the door in a deliberate movement, as if she was taking the package straight to the police. Betty ran after her and grabbed at her again. 'Chris! Don't, please!'

'If you won't help yourself, how can I help you?'

'I don't see how it would help. If I did...what you want.'

'You have to take my word for it.'

Betty took a deep breath. 'What...what would I have to do?' Her voice showed no sign that she was giving way. But Christine seemed to know that she had won the battle. She smiled lovingly at her sister and her voice was gentle, reassuring.

'Trust me. That's all. Have complete faith in me.'

'I do trust you, Chris. Whatever you say. Only I'm...scared.'

'No need to be. Honestly, there's nothing to be scared of.'

'But I don't know anything about it.'

'You will by the time the initiation ceremony is over. Just do what I say.'

'Is it true that...they're naked? Would I have to be naked too?'

'It's just a simple ceremony. Beautiful. All you have to do is to keep your mind on afterwards. On getting Johnny back. Now forget about it and stop worrying. All right?'

Betty's silence was the nearest she would come to agreeing. Christine opened the door to leave. Gerald was standing outside. He put up his hand as if had just arrived and was about to knock.

'Just coming to thank you for getting Sybil to have a rest.'

Christine closed the door behind her and walked with Gerald along the landing. 'How is she?'

'She's sleeping. That's what she needs. Has your sister got over her boyfriend trouble?'

'Yes, she has now. And I've got good news. She's agreed to be initiated.'

Gerald's eyes gleamed with anticipation. 'That is splendid. Well done, Christine. Well done indeed!'

'I think you should make her one of your drinks. We don't want her changing her mind.' Christine heard herself saying it as an order.

And Gerald accepted it. 'Certainly. I'll make it up right away.'

'One moment!' He stopped in his tracks at this word of command. He turned slowly. It was quite incredible how this young girl had changed overnight. She had matured, developed authority. The sense of power she now conveyed could not be ignored. And he had no wish to ignore it. He was happy to let her have the reins - for the time being. It was quite amusing. 'Betty is to be my sacrifice. Mine!'

The smile vanished instantly from Gerald's face. This he hadn't expected. 'Does the High Priestess know?' he asked.

'She won't be there.' It was a plain statement of fact. There was no question of doubt.

Gerald knew exactly what she meant. He smiled again as they reached the staircase. A glance was exchanged. Nothing more needed to be said.

Deep in the neglected ground which fell away behind the house, Sybil struggled through the overgrown vegetation towards an old barn. Now that she was near enough to make it out against the dusk-laden sky, she snatched impatiently at tentacles of wild creepers trailing from the trees. Once or twice she stumbled as her feet were tripped by tendrils of ivy which carpeted the ground. But nothing deterred her from staggering on towards her objective. Her eyes were fixed ahead, the barn's black mass now loomed above her, encompassing her as she dragged one of its rickety double-doors open. It scraped along the ground, its rusted hinges no longer holding it to swing freely. She pushed impatiently to make a sufficient opening to squeeze through.

Her arrival disturbed hundreds of bats, hanging eerily in the vaulted roof. She moved to the centre of the empty barn, almost losing her stance on the sun-starved earth, which in consequence was veneered with rancid soil.

The bats fluttered and quietened down again like some weird audience settling itself before the start of an ethereal performance. Sybil raised her arms in supplication, tears blackened with mascara ran down her cheeks, her forehead was creased with lines of pain.

Her lips mouthed the words 'Help me! Help me!' She waited for a response. None came. With a great effort she spoke the words hoarsely 'Help me! Help me!' Some of the bats fluttered, but that was all.

She looked around the darkness, searching with her eyes and her ears for some signal, some sign of a reply. Some guidance, some intelligible response, hoped for, desperately needed. Nothing was forthcoming. She screamed in panic-stricken fury. 'Help me! Oh, help me! Please!' The bats, disturbed by the high vibrations of her screeched words, fell from the roof into flight. They swooped down, filling the whole of the barn, whirling around Sybil. She stood helpless, motionless, allowing herself to be buffeted and her hair whipped and caught by the wings of the blind creatures.

The fury of their high-speed gyrations created a maelstrom of sound around her and she screamed again in anguish.

Now she began to wave her arms, aggravating the bats' movements and causing more of them to crash into her. Was this the sign she was looking for? Were they sympathetic creatures? She began to believe they were and tore off her clothes so that she could feel every impact on her naked skin.

She braced herself against the blows, her legs and arms apart, as if to catch the maximum impact from as many of the creatures as she could. Direct collisions heightened the masochistic ecstasy in her eyes. These were creatures of darkness, as she was herself. Were they also the instruments of the Evil Master from whom she was so desperately seeking renewed strength and increased powers?

She screamed and screamed until her throat was so hoarse it could make no more sound. She tried to keep up the excitement by flailing her arms. But the bats were becoming used to her presence and the leaders were beginning to resettle. Soon they were all hanging again, swinging silently from the old rafters as if nothing had happened.

Sybil subsided, her blotched body a legacy of the bombardment. With a last effort she stared up at the roof, as if seeing through it to the night sky and infinity. She was back where she came in, only able to mouth without sound 'Please help me! Please! Please help me!' But still there was no response.

The same infinite sky, taking its first gentle glow from the newly-risen mood, was a canopy for the garden where Christine stood by the sundial, pensive, enjoying the scented night air. Once or twice she thought she heard a distant cry, but it was orchestrated with night sounds from the woods and did no more than add another instrument to nature's symphony.

Two arms snaked around her waist from behind and locked

her in an embrace. She did not move. 'Peter?'

'How did you know it was me?' Peter kissed her ear.

'I recognise the feel of those arms. Remember?'

'Could I forget? So soon?'

'And this night! It's a wonderful night. Look at the moon. Listen to the sounds from the woods.'

Peter looked straight at Christine. 'When the moon shines in your eyes, how can I look at the moon itself?'

'Mmmm. I like that. Quite a poet, Peter.'

Peter came round to face her, still encircling her waist. 'That's the last thing I am. But you're looking so...so...well, beautiful. There's no other word for it. Yes, there is. Radiant, that's even better.'

'Maybe it's because I'm happy.'

Peter thought she meant being with him and fished. 'Any special reason?'

'Yes. I'm just beginning to realise what it means to be a witch. What power it gives you.'

Peter was disappointed but not deterred. He did not take her interest in witchcraft seriously. He remembered how he had found it a fascinating novelty but he'd soon got over it. He shook her playfully by the waist. 'You've got quite enough power without bothering about witchcraft.' He pulled her close. 'What you do to me is power enough for anyone.'

He held her tight to him. She could feel his legs brace as he pressed himself against her.

'No, Peter. Not now.'

'Chris! This time it will be all right.'

'I know!'

'Well then?'

Christine sensed that she was weakening. She must not give in, much as she was enjoying feeling what she was doing to him. Peter found that he no longer needed the pressure of his arms on her back. She was holding him just as tightly. He forced his hands between their bodies to caress her breasts, which were splayed apart with the force of the embrace.

'No, Peter! We must wait!'

Peter detected the lack of conviction in her voice. This time, for once - oh, please God, for once - give him the strength to dominate. To exert his will over another.

'No. Now!' he pleaded.

'Later,' Christine was kissing him, yet trying to pull his hands away, her arms, vice-like on his wrists. Still, she pressed herself against him, with as much force as he bored at her.

'Peter! Don't spoil it. Don't spoil everything. It will be even better later on.' She was fighting herself as much as him, struggling against sensual excitement his caresses aroused in her.

'When? When d'you mean?' His mouth was warm and urgent, on her cheeks, her ears, her neck.

'At the ceremony. The Sabbat.'

Peter was so astonished that he pulled back a little to search her eyes. 'You and me? At the ceremony?'

'Why not?'

'Well okay - why not? I'm game. But...how?'

Christine tipped up her chin. She had a natural flair for what an actress would call a good exit line.

'Because...tonight...I shall be High Priestess.'

And before he could recover from this shock announcement, she had planted a light kiss on the tip of his nose and run off out of sight.

Peter was about to follow but thought better of it and turned towards the house. Well, at least he had her promise. He should have taken her in the boathouse. He could kick himself for missing that chance. She was hot for him then. Now he couldn't avoid a sneaking suspicion that things would never again be like their first session together. Already things had changed. Now he was the supplicant. Christine was in command.

Johnny never walked anywhere if he could help it. Now he'd walked all the way from the local. But he needed that. He'd left the Jaguar in front of the Witch's Broomstick and here he was for some reason, enjoying the night air and strolling down a country lane. And instead of oxygenating the alcohol, it seemed to have sobered him up. Funny!

Why he was walking he hadn't the faintest idea. Never mind, it made a change. And gave you time to think. But he couldn't keep his mind on working out a plan of action. Or explain to himself why he was walking in this direction? Or why he had turned down this lane at the cross-roads. Then he realised he had subconsciously returned to Wychwold - to where Betty was.

'Hello Johnny!'

'Blimey!'

Christine was standing in the gateway as if waiting for him. 'Christine! Well, I'll be blowed! Just the one I want to see.'

'I've been expecting you too.'

'You what?'

'It doesn't matter. Why do you want to see me? Let's get that over first.'

'I want to get things straight between us.'

'Good. So do I.'

'Yes. Well, you've only heard Betty's side. I don't want to cause a rift between you two. Be silly, wouldn't it, when you're so close. Twins and all that. But I don't like the idea of her hanging around this place. She's not like you. Nothing personal. You know what I mean?'

'I know what you mean. But she doesn't want to go. Didn't she tell you that?'

'Only because she promised she'd stay with you. That's Betty all over. She wouldn't break a promise for anything. Now, if you'd release her from it, it'd be quite different. She'd come with me like a shot. Now. Right this moment. You just see if she wouldn't!'

'No, she wouldn't. She doesn't want to now. Quite apart from her promise to me.'

Johnny began to get uppity. 'You think you can make her do just what you want. All right, maybe you can, at present. But it's going to stop.'

'Who's going to stop it? You?'

'Yes. Me. I'm having her out of that house tonight. Promise or no promise.'

'What's the hurry?'

'I've heard things.'

'What things?'

'Funny old things. If you ask me, they're all freaked out down here. You may be able to cope, but I'm worried about Betty.'

'Take her back tomorrow then.'

'I'm not waiting for tomorrow, thanks. I'm taking her right now.'

And he strode purposefully past Christine down the drive.

Christine turned and called after him very cool, very calm, but accusing. 'So you think you're more suitable to look after her, do you? A cheap little drug-pusher and pimp?'

Johnny swung round at her, shocked at her knowledge. He ran back, shaping up to hit her. Christine did not flinch. She smiled; secure in her ascendancy over him.

'The police will be very interested in how you tried to push drugs on Betty. She's not eighteen yet. That makes it double trouble for you, doesn't it?'

'You wouldn't tell them, Chris? You wouldn't?'

'When you've been trying to corrupt my sister? It's vile.'

'I'm not trying to corrupt her. Let me explain.'

'Every pusher has an explanation when he's caught. Always! The same old story!'

'You are going to tell them, aren't you? I can see it in your eyes. Just to get at me, you're going to involve Betty. You don't care.'

Christine's eyes flashed. 'I do care. I care more for Betty than anyone in this world.'

'Then why shop me? If it's going to involve her?'

'I didn't say I would. You did.'

'Then let me tell you the truth.'

'I wouldn't believe it - whatever you said. Clever excuses are all part of the game, aren't they?'

'No point in trying then, is there?'

'None at all. But I'm not having Betty mixed up in that racket. Understand?'

'She's not mixed up in it. I wouldn't let anything happen to her through me. What do you think I am?'

'You put the stuff on her.'

'Only to keep for me. Exactly what I told her at the time. You don't seem to mind her getting mixed up with the weirdies in this place.'

'They're not weirdies.'

'What are these goings-on then?'

'I'm not going into details. You wouldn't understand, anyway. It's important to me. I'll see she comes to no harm.'

'Good.'

'That's better. Now, you do as I say, and I won't go to the police. That's a fair exchange.'

'You like to get your own way, don't you?'

Christine nodded her head. Her smile was of complete confidence. 'If you really want to help Betty, you'll listen to me. If you really care for her.'

Johnny glared at her. Stubborn. His jaw set firmly. 'Course I care for her.'

There was a silence. Each measured the other. Their eyes locked in mute combat. Neither was prepared to give. Stalemate had been reached.

Sybil looked terrible. She staggered along the river bank, meandering and swaying like a drunk. Only the way she pressed her fingers to her temples and the anguish etched deep on her face indicated she was not intoxicated - not by alcohol. Her eyes were wild, staring. Anyone seeing her could have been forgiven for thinking she really was possessed of the Devil. But there was nobody to see her. Nobody to call for assistance. The river bank was deserted and dark. As unwelcoming now as it was idyllic in sunlight. In the distance, a summer storm grumbled. Lightening forked down the sky. The river chattered on.

Once or twice she nearly overbalanced into the river. She had lost her shoes and her clothes were stained with the slime of the rancid barn floor. Her face was blotchy from the impact of the bats and her hair was dishevelled. She looked around frantically, still mouthing: 'Help me! Help me!' Still hoping for a sign of succour. From time to time, moans of pain aped her.

Suddenly her eyes cleared. She stood still for a moment. She was remembering the ceremony. The time for it must be approaching. As if impelled, she turned and ran straight as an arrow in the direction of the house.

Cars were parking in front of the house, moonlight and the distant lightning making their bodywork gleam. Members of the coven gravitated to the front door, some already gowned and hooded. Others, carrying cases, began robing in the hall.

In the cellar, Gerald, ready in his scarlet robes, was making a final check-up of the items to be used in the ceremony. He had a few last minute words with the drummer. He looked at his watch and nodded to the man. Quietly but insistently, the practised fingers began to drum on the taut skins, beating out the summons. Gerald set a taper to the tall black candles and the joss sticks. Gently, undramatically, he was creating an ambience of witchcraft with a few skilled touches.

After a final survey that all was ready, he climbed the stone steps to welcome the coven gathering in the hall.

Staring out of her bedroom window at the arrivals had done

nothing to help Betty fight off the fast-growing apprehension she felt. Her bare legs trembled, although the summer night was warm. Christine had told her to get undressed and go to bed - nothing else. Betty had trusted her so far but now she wished that Chris had explained a little of what was to happen, given her at least some clue to go on. She wrapped her dressing gown more tightly around her shivering body.

Sybil reached the house by the kitchen door and slipped up the back stairs unnoticed. If anyone had seen her appearance, they would have thought she had miraculously come through some fantastic accident. Once in her room she made straight for the shower, dropping her ruined clothes in a trail behind her. She turned the tap on full and stood with her eyes closed as the cool, cleansing water flooded over her.

Although the window was closed, Betty still shivered. She saw a freshening breeze bend the trees in its path. The distant thunder seemed to vibrate down the length of her spine. She spun round anxiously as she heard the door open. And gasped to see Christine in her white witch robes. Could she appear before all these people looking so beautiful and virginal, and patently nude underneath the clinging silky material? Betty realised she was feeling envy, an emotion she had never experienced before. Christine came to Betty, took both her hands and gazed deep into her eyes. Betty wavered and looked away. 'Chris, I can't go through with it.'

'You can! Of course you can. I'm the High Priestess tonight. So nothing can hurt you or go wrong. You don't need this.'

Christine removed Betty's dressing gown, never allowing her eyes to move from her sister's. 'And stop trembling! I've told you - you won't get hurt.'

'I wish I was dead.'

'Quite the opposite. This is where you start living. I promise you, you're going to thank me afterwards.'

Christine noticed Betty was wearing her briefs under her night-dress. 'I said get ready for bed. You don't sleep in those.'

Christine pulled up Betty's night-dress. Betty drew back.

'No, Chris! Let me. Please.'

But Christine's eyes held Betty under their domination. Her hands grasped the top of the briefs and pulled them down. Betty submitted so passively that Christine had to kneel and lift each trembling foot in turn before the briefs were entirely removed. Christine threw them carelessly on to the bed.

Betty sighed. 'What are they going to do with me? Nobody's ever taken my clothes off before.'

'They? They're going to do nothing, absolutely nothing. Don't be frightened! I'll make it go right. Look at me, Betty - and trust me. Just remember that. Look at me!'

Betty stared at her. Christine held her hands and they stood, like statues, for a few moments. Gradually Betty's trembling subsided. Her body relaxed. Her eyes took on a slightly glazed look. She did not move them from Christine's gaze. Christine smiled, satisfied. Gently, she led her sister from the room.

The candles were flickering. The music began to throb loudly. The monkish figures were forming the circle. Now Christine seemed to be pulling rather than leading Betty as they moved into the chapel. But Betty's resistance was minimal, almost token, and her eyes were fixed, already dreamlike.

When the twins stood side by side in front of the altar, Gerald faced them and raised his hands. 'Blessed be!' There was a murmur from the assembled group as they bowed their heads to accept the benediction.

Gerald detached Christine's hand from Betty's and took her towards the Chair of Office. Suddenly the chapel door swung open. It was Sybil, robed, head consciously held high, a majestic contrast to the pathetic figure on the river bank. Taking a deep breath, she moved to her usual position.

'I said I would be here tonight.' Quietly but firmly she spoke for Christine's benefit.

Gerald glanced at Christine, his expression troubled. Then, filled with remorse to have to let himself be swayed so completely by this young girl, he moved to Sybil's side.

Sybil was cold and poised. 'Is the initiate ready?' Without waiting for an answer she moved to Betty, who looked to be in a dream, not knowing what was really going on.

The inspection was quick but all-embracing. Sybil's sharp

eyes took Betty in from head to foot. She delighted to see the girl helpless and submissive in front of her. She turned to the altar and reached for the gold chalice. Her facade was momentarily betrayed as her hand shook and a little oil spilled over the lip on to the white lace altar cloth. Gerald watched her anxiously. His eyes turned to Christine. Yes, she had seen it too. She seemed to nod to him slightly. Then she moved to Betty, alone before the altar. Christine began to unfasten the night-dress buttons at the nape of her neck. Then she swept her hands down her sister's shoulders taking the night-dress with them until it fell to the ground.

Sybil lifted her chin resolutely and commanded in a whisper: 'Step forward.' The naked figure of Betty obediently moved a pace towards Gerald, one step taking her clear of the silky material on the stone floor. Gerald's mouth was dry. The girl was as beautiful as her sister. More delicate - and even more desirable for that.

Sybil moved towards the pale, naked body with the chalice. Christine watched like a hawk ready to counter-strike. From her position, beside but slightly behind her sister, she could see Sybil's slightest move. And Sybil could see her watchful eyes. This had the effect Christine desired. Sybil's hand began to shake as she raised the chalice. She nearly dropped it. Oil spilled onto Betty's feet. Gerald moved quickly to take the chalice away, but Sybil resisted him. 'No. I am the High Priestess.'

She stared defiantly at Christine, but the time when she could dominate the girl had gone. For ever, Christine's eyes pierced Sybil's. The High Priestess tried to break away but found her dark pupils tied to Christine's by invisible unbreakable thread.

Sybil started to sway as if she was dizzy. Gerald, amazed to see Christine gradually dominating the scene, awaited the outcome of the battle. He was both intrigued and yet resigned to the outcome. The rhythm was building up to a crescendo and this seemed to give extra power to Christine, while Sybil was becoming overwhelmed by the incessant beat.

As Sybil began to crumble, Christine moved to her. But she did not prevent her from dropping to the ground in a heap. At first

transfixed by the beautiful naked body of his love. He tried to reassure Betty by whispering 'I love you, I love you,' over and over and over again. Her eyes flickered, then a smile of happiness lit up her face, and he knew that she had recognised him even through her hypnotic state. He knelt beside her, kissing her, his hands gently caressing the sleek oiled body. Betty's expression was radiant. Johnny was there and she knew he loved her.

Seeing the sacrifice now inviting initiation, the circle began gyrating to the crescendo of pulsating drum beats. Nobody gave even a casual glance at the figure in the background. Sybil crouched even further into the shadows as she watched, realising she was helpless and forgotten.

The rhythm grew frenetic as the climax approached. Whirling naked bodies flung themselves round the chapel as Johnny hesitantly mounted the altar and lowered himself onto Betty. Her arms went round him as soon as their bodies met.

They were oblivious to the rest of the ceremony. Johnny was moving into her sweetly. Betty accepted him with complete trust. She gave a little cry. Johnny stopped immediately. He searched her eyes for signs of pain but all he saw was love, urging him to move further home.

This time it was Betty murmuring 'I love you.' He replied with a kiss which tongued their mouths together. They were doubly interlocked, crested on waves of joy to an intimate Paradise, where no one else existed.

Christine felt a stab of awareness. Betty's kind of Paradise was something she would never know - absolute love for the man who was taking her, an ecstasy of giving. She was happy for Betty, genuinely happy. And not too regretful for herself. After all, she had power. That meant more to her - so much more. And she had achieved it tonight.

She felt a gentle touch on her arm and found Peter beside her. He held out his arms, mutely asking for fulfilment of the promise she had made him earlier. She smiled. Then slowly she stepped down from the dais and allowed him to disrobe her. He held her close against his own naked body. They began to move, faster, faster still, in time to the beating bongos, in a ballet movement with the rest of the coven.

But the pulsating noise and the spectacular gymnastics of the group was only a tawdry background. The altar where the young couple made love with such tender, flowering beauty dominated the scene. Betty began to moan, until suddenly she was making the only sounds in the room. The drummer was exhausted and silent. The coven members had spent their force and sunk to the floor. Her voice made ethereal sounds of indescribable joy which echoed from the stone walls.

They watched, open-mouthed in envy, as Betty cried out Johnny's name, their bodies moving in unison. He too was murmuring now and his gasps of fulfilment found a response in every man that watched.

Then Johnny and Betty dropped limp together. They lay still.

Betty's arms slid from his back and hung over the sides of the altar. Johnny used his to press himself up.

Still nobody moved as he climbed down from the altar, gathered Betty in his arms and carried her from the dais across the circle, cutting it in two, as the members parted, past a speechless Sybil, out through the door, and up the cellar steps. Betty hung in his arms, still in her Paradise, murmuring his name.

Christine walked a few paces behind them but stopped when she came face to face with Sybil. 'Leave the chapel,' she commanded firmly.

Sybil summoned what strength she had left. She shook her head. 'No.'

'Very well,' Christine threatened. She turned her back and looked at Gerald. 'Form the Circle,' she ordered.

Gerald did not move. But Peter did. He joined hands with the people either side of him. Others began to follow suit. Christine joined in to make the circle complete. Only Gerald and Sybil stood outside it.

Christine's voice commanded them again: 'Tonight we have power! Tonight we will reach the heights! Follow me.'

The members of the circle watched as she slowly lowered herself onto her haunches and crouched so low that her beautiful breasts rested on her knees. First one, then another, sank down into the same position. Christine closed her eyes for a moment, gathering strength. When they opened, they had that familiar glazed look. She was going into a trance. She swayed and the circle followed suit. She moved inwards. The ring became tighter and tighter, naked bodies pressing on each other until there was a ring of writhing, sensuous flesh. Arms, legs, all parts of their bodies twisting and intertwined each other in a paroxysm of movement.

Gerald and Sybil at opposite ends of the chapel, were unwilling voyeurs of a multi-orgasm. But this was only a prelude to what Christine intended to accomplish.

Johnny carried Betty across the lawn to the base of the fountain, still spurting water into the balmy night air. He lowered her onto the ribboned grass below the fantails of a massive cedar tree and knelt beside her.

He looked at her, wonderingly, almost afraid to touch her - yet filled with an overpowering protectiveness and love towards her. 'All right?' he enquired. He had to know whether he had hurt her, emotionally or physically. A breathless whisper gave him the answer he wanted. 'Perfect. Absolutely perfect.'

She put her arms around his neck but after a moment he took them away. She looked up at him, bewildered.

'Betty! Darling, we must talk. It's important. We must get things sorted out. Then we can treat all that like a bad dream.'

'Bad dream? Beautiful dream. Except I hope it wasn't a dream at all. So it can happen again. Whenever we want it to. You will want to again, Johnny - won't you?'

'Of course! And I don't want anything to spoil it from now on. That's why we must talk!'

She pulled a face and nuzzled her cheek against him.

'Must we? Why?'

''Cos we got to face it now. Not later.'

'Face what?'

Johnny chose his words carefully. He had to bring himself to the point gradually. 'That packet I asked you to keep for me?'

A look of alarm crossed Betty's face. She'd forgotten all about that in her new found happiness.

'Where is it, Betty?'

'In our room. I brought it in my bag, I didn't want to leave it behind. You said to keep it safe.'

'That's right. You didn't look inside, did you?'

'No, I didn't, but...' She couldn't bring herself to say it.

'But Chris did. I know.'

Betty was bewildered until Johnny explained about the confrontation with Christine. 'She accused me of pushing the stuff. And getting you involved. Do you think I'd do a thing like that? To you?'

'No! I said you wouldn't, Johnny. I told her.'

'That's what I wanted to hear. More than anything.' He looked down at her, a great tenderness filling his being. He wrapped his arms around her and kissed her, on her eyes, her upturned nose and her mouth. After a moment, she sighed happily. 'But what are you doing with it? You don't have to tell me if you don't want to. But I'd like to put things right with Chris.'

'I collect it for Abby. Then I store it till she wants it. That way she can't be caught with the stuff on her.'

'But you could be!'

'I know. But I'm nobody, am I? And I've been lucky. Anyway, it's all over now. When I think I might have lost you because of it -'

She put her finger on his lips. 'Well, you haven't.'

'I'm finished with Abby. Someone else can fix her up with cars. Won't ever see her again. Okay? Then we can make a fresh start together.'

'We?' Betty put her arms around his neck again. Only now did she become aware they were naked. She looked down at her breasts, flattened against Johnny's bony chest.

'Yes. We. We'll get married. Soon as we can. Why not?'

'You still want me?'

'Well, after seeing me lying there. I'd no idea it was going to be you, Johnny. I hope you don't think I didn't care who it was. I just couldn't move - or do anything to get away.'

'Chris told me you were going through all that for my sake. The two-faced bitch!'

'She was trying to help. Don't you see?'

'Trying to help! Who? You?' He snorted with disgust. 'She was doing it for her own sake, darling. Make no mistake. She'll do anything to get her own way. And she doesn't mind who gets hurt in the process.'

'Johnny, don't say things like that.'

'Well, it's true. I don't care if she is your sister. Look how's she's got herself hooked up in this witch business. And for what? To get her where she wants to be - a big success. She's so bloody ambitious, I reckon she'd do murder for it, if necessary.'

Betty was thoughtful. Looking back, so much of Johnny's logic made sense. 'I suppose you could be right. I wouldn't be surprised at anything Chris did, she's so single-minded. Always has been.'

'No good will come of it. Mark my words.'

Betty's arms were still locked around him. 'That's her world. We have our own to think about.'

Johnny kissed her gently, but long. She dropped her hands from the nape of his neck and ran them outstretched along the grass.

'Johnny, you realise we are stark naked?'

'Yes, I did have some sort of idea.'

'That's something Chris has done for me. I could never have been like this, before tonight. I never knew how marvellous it would feel. You and me, and absolutely nothing between us.'

'I'd have taught you myself. In my own way. If you'd let me.'

'But would I have let you? Remember that day at your Mum's. I was a different girl.'

Johnny kissed her again, not quite so gently. Her whole body quivered as she waited for him.

'Then it was true? I didn't dream it?'

Johnny put his mouth close to her ear, his lips brushing it as he whispered: 'Would you like me to make sure?'

'How can I be sure? It was all so...out of this world.'

'Let's hope it'll always be out of this world! But no audience, eh? Never again. This time it's for us alone.'

He began to kiss her, and caress her slowly. And then with more and more urgency.

'You've no idea what you're doing to me,' she breathed. 'Inside.'

Once more that sharp ecstatic pain which made her wince and yet not want him to stop. As he raised his head and his lips returned to hers, she felt him slide on top of her.

The stars brightened, shimmering and sparkling in competition with her eyes. A shooting star traced across the sky and sped through the midnight blackness.

Johnny needed no bidding. He looked into her eyes and saw the pupils rolling slowly up under her limp eyelids. She was ascending into Paradise again. And so was he.

Christine grew tall from the centre of the writhing bodies, as she stretched her arms towards the chapel ceiling, as if being drawn up by the tips of her fingers. The entangled flesh around her feet began to unwind as she incantated: 'High. High. High.'

Slowly and softly at first, the group followed her example, picking up the chant and echoing the words after her. Gradually her voice grew more incisive, her face upturned to the stuffed bats, the 'High. High. High' almost vibrating the rafters.

Gradually the flesh separated, but the bodies kept close as they slowly stood, their arms upstretched like Christine's. They bunched into a pyramid of flesh, Christine at its apex.

As the words rebounded round the chapel, they seemed to disturb Sybil's atrophied mind. Suddenly she turned to face the door. Gerald held out his hand as if to restrain her, but the 'High, High. High' dominated her. The chorus repeated Christine's shrieking staccato words. Sybil was at its mercy.

'High! High! High!'

It propelled Sybil from behind as she slowly mounted the stone steps towards the hall. At each new triplet, she moved a step higher.

Betty and Johnny were floating amongst the stars. Time and place had no meaning. Nothing could pull them asunder. Both were in ecstasy; both trying their utmost to achieve it for the other. That was their secret. That was the ultimate satisfaction, knowing it to be super-natural for both, neither one using or dominating the other. It was the difference between love and just plain sex.

On the altar Betty had dreamed it was like this. Now she was fulfilling her dream. Her arms were tight around her lover. This time she was not dreaming. She was aware - oh, so marvellously aware, aware.

Still afloat in the stars, but now afloat inside too. Then as the magic fountains subsided, they fell gently back to earth. She felt the dewy grass on her bare back for the first time for an age. He felt the night air on his and sighed into her wide-open mouth. Their bodies stayed coupled. Limp, exhausted, satisfied, heart-pounding bodies. Locked together in the magic of natural love.

Sybil reached to the top landing of the main staircase. But the chant of 'High! High! High!' seemed no further away. Clearer, if anything. She moved in slow-motion towards the iron spiral of the fire escape, which led out of the attic on to the roof, and began moving upwards once more.

The pyramid of bodies was still urging: 'High! High! High!' But Christine was not satisfied.

'We are losing strength.'

'High! High! High! 'Sybil's steps grew slower.

'We are losing strength!' Although the whole house from cellar to rooftop now separated them, Christine knew her power was weakening. And suddenly she knew why.

'We are only twelve.' She looked hard at Gerald and com-manded him: 'Join the circle!' Gerald stood apart. He wanted to leave the chapel, but something compelled him to stay.

'High! High! High!' Sybil could barely lift her foot to the next step. Only three steps to go and she had come almost to a stop.

In the cellar below, Gerald tried to fight back at Christine. He knew at last what she was trying to do. 'I won't make thir-teen. It's wrong. Evil.' He made another effort to keep away from the pyramid.

'I'm the High Priestess! I command you. Join the circle!'

'High! High! High!'

Gerald felt himself drawn towards his own circle against his will. 'No! It's the Black Arts. It's evil.'

'Join the circle!'

Christine held out her hand to Gerald. He kept his arms resolutely at his side, fighting a desperate inner battle against the power this extraordinary girl wielded.

High above them Sybil had one foot on the top step. The door was open to the roof. Now she stopped altogether, no power willing her to go on.

Christine stared into Gerald's eyes. Her voice, though quiet, was very clear. 'Join the circle, I tell you.'

She pushed bodies away from her as if to make a space. Again she held out her hand. Gerald felt his last resistance draining away. He stepped forward. Christine grasped him tightly, as she pulled him into the human pyramid.

Gerald resigned himself that he was helpless to resist. Her fingers gripped him tighter. 'Your hands, Gerald. Raise your hands.' Gerald's hands went up.

'High! High! High!' Gerald's lips moved but no sound emerged.

As the chant screeched from the others, Christine gripped him in pulses, as if her hands could squeeze the words from his lips.

'High! High! High!' Thirteen voices at last, shrieked to the top of the building. Sybil began to move forward again, out into the night, to the edge of the roof.

Christine's eyes blazed as she released her hold on Gerald and broke from the pyramid to snatch the dagger from the altar. She whipped out the blade and stood before the altar, grasping the hilt in both hands and raising it as high as she could reach. Her head fell back so far it seemed her neck must break. Her flashing eyes searched beyond the dagger, beyond the chapel ceiling, up through the house to the roof.

Sybil was poised on the ledge, her bare feet now keeping only a tenuous balance between life and death.

Betty lay on the grass, her eyes misty with joy. Johnny asked her: 'Happy?'

She nodded. He slipped his hand around her to draw her up

to meet his kiss. But suddenly she gave a start of horror.

'Johnny! Look!'

He turned sharply to where she was pointing.

On the roof, in stark silhouette, Sybil swayed on the very edge, her robe open and blowing behind her in the night breeze.

Johnny leaped up and hared across the lawn. As he ran, he shouted frantically. 'No! Wait! Don't move!'

Christine's face glowed with success. 'She is there. There!' And with every ounce of strength in her body, she plunged the dagger down past her breasts with such force that it buried itself deep in the altar top.

Betty ran after Johnny. But as he neared the house, Sybil jumped, plunging down to the path like the dagger to the altar. Betty felt the thud of the impact under her feet. And felt sick.

Christine turned from the altar and faced the silent twelve. Her face was wan, drained with exhaustion.

'The Evil One has had his sacrifice. Blessed be!'

Eleven of the group repeated 'Blessed be!' Gerald was silent, looking at Christine in the same way Frankenstein eventually came to see his homicidal monster.

Johnny got up from examining Sybil's body and turned just in time to catch Betty. He pulled her away and buried her head on his chest. She knew from the way he held her that Sybil was dead.

They were taking the sign down at the Sybil Waite Studio. Passers-by who watched it being loaded on to the shopfitter's van wondered what new business was going to take its place. Shops come and go in the King's Road. Yesterday's boutique was tomorrow's trattoria. The ever-changing street.

Some shook their heads. They remembered the report of the inquest in the papers. Why she should have taken her own life at the height of her career was a mystery the Coroner's Court failed to solve.

There was a party in full swing at the time. Two of the guests were in the grounds and testified they saw her jump of her own volition, from the roof of Wychwold. She definitely jumped. And the owner and one of the guests, a photographer, had stated that everyone else was downstairs. No one was able to throw any light on when she left the gathering or why she should be so depressed as to take this terrible step.

'Took her life, whilst the balance of her mind was disturbed,' seemed the only possibly verdict.

Johnny and Betty ran down the steps of the Registry Office. London traffic whizzed past the kerb. Proudly, Johnny took his new wife's arm and with a grand gesture, opened the door of a shining red sports car parked nearby.

'Johnny! You don't mean...' she gasped, eyes alight with wonder.

'Always told you I was a good salesman, doll!' he grinned. 'Even sold this one to myself! It's my wedding present - to both of us.'

She ran her hand along the polished paintwork in a thrill of ownership. 'But can we afford it?' she asked in a sudden apprehension.

Johnny grinned at her. 'From now on, Mrs Dixon, you leave the financial worries to me.'

There was a hoot of laughter from behind them. Their friends had gathered on the pavement; a few of Johnny's and one or two of Betty's who had been able to make the journey. They showered them with confetti. Johnny pulled a face. 'Oh, that's nice, that is! You promised you wouldn't -'

'Where are you going for your honeymoon?' came an excited question.

'Don't think I'm telling you lot, do you?' Johnny shouted back. 'Specially after this!' And he threw a handful of confetti at the offender. 'Hop in, Baby, and let's get the hell out of here!'

They scrambled into the car. Betty being embraced last of all by her father. After pecking her a kiss he yelled at Johnny: 'Take good care of her. Or you'll have me to answer to.' And he slammed the door without waiting for a reply.

For a moment, Johnny was absorbed in weaving through the traffic. Betty stared ahead thoughtfully, not really seeing anything. He shot a sideways glance at her and smiled. 'What's up?'

'Nothing,' she smiled back. 'Just, I didn't think he'd come, you know. Funny chap, our Dad.'

'I told you he would if you invited him. Besides, we didn't

want him turning nasty, forbidding the banns.'

'We'd only have to wait a little longer. I'm eighteen next month.'

'Couldn't wait a minute let alone a month. In case someone else came along and pinched you off me!'

He took her hand and squeezed it, then raised it to his mouth. A sharp hoot from the car behind brought his attention back to the road.

'It didn't bother you - Christine not coming?'

She shook her head. 'Not really. She could've done if she'd wanted to. She can't be that busy.'

'I wondered. Me - I don't care if we never see her again - but you, well, you were so close all those years.'

Betty nodded her head gravely. 'Funny when you think of it. We weren't a bit alike, in spite of being twins. I suppose we'll go our own ways from now on. Somehow, it doesn't matter. Now I've got you.'

'And I've got you, my little darling.'

They turned to look deep into each other's eyes till Johnny had to wrench his away again because of the traffic.

'If you only knew how bad I want to kiss you,' he muttered from the side of his mouth.

She giggled. 'Here, Johnny?'

'Here, there, anywhere. You're my wife. I'm entitled, aren't I?'

'My wife.' Betty felt a glow of warmth and love flood through her at the words. Christine could have her success, her glamorous life, her money. Nothing could match her own happiness. Ever.

Miss Fletcher was trying to stave off a persistent caller. She gripped the telephone tighter, her voice sharpened. 'I'm sorry. My instructions are to make no more engagements. Not even for top newspapermen. Miss Lane is extremely busy. She is seeing no one. No one at all.'

The telephone journalist didn't heed a word. 'Look,' he continued. 'Doesn't she want the publicity? I'm doing this series on the big wheels of tomorrow. Now if she'd rather I wrote up someone else as the most likely to become the new Sybil Waite, okay. But when a throne is vacant the Press has some say in who sits in it. Just because she's taken over the premises, it doesn't follow -'

Miss Fletcher knew that if she didn't interrupt he'd never stop. 'I'll tell Miss Lane everything you say.'

'Weren't you Sybil Waite's secretary? I seem to recognise your voice.'

'Miss Lane very kindly took me on. I don't see what that's got to do with it. Miss Lane has only returned from New York this very morning. She has the time change to get adjusted to, and a backlog of work and appointments. I'm very sorry. Good day.'

She tried to put the telephone down without slamming it, almost successfully. She sighed and made a note of the call. A young girl came in at that moment. Miss Fletcher only needed half a glance to tell why she was there. Yet another would-be model, copying the top-girl she thought she resembled. Hair-do, fashion, make-up and a cheap imitation of the latest shoes. And, of course, the inevitable low neckline in case it was a man who could help her. Couldn't be more than sixteen, surely!

'I'd like to see Miss Lane.' Her voice was uptight.

'Have you an appointment?' Miss Fletcher knew very well she hadn't.

'No, but I've just arrived from Manchester. Someone said she was looking for girls like me.'

'Miss Lane can't possibly see anyone. She's out.'

'I don't mind waiting.' The voice betrayed that she had nowhere particularly to go. As if Miss Fletcher didn't know.

'There's really no point. Miss Lane only sees girls by appointment.'

'Maybe if she comes in, she could see me just for a minute. That's all I want. Just to see me.'

The girl sank onto the leather settee. Miss Fletcher knew that if she made her leave then and there, the near-hysterics would erupt into tears. She decided to leave it for a few minutes with the warning: 'I've no idea whether she'll even be back today.' The girl seemed not to hear, but stared at her vacantly.

The shopfitters were screwing down the new sign to replace The Sybil Waite Studio. Passers-by noted - some of them with a knowing look - that it read - The Christina Lane Studio. In exactly the same lettering. Didn't she give evidence at the inquest? Saying how much Miss Waite had done for her career? That she was the last person in the world to take her own life?'

Peter had a quick look at the sign and ran up the stairs. 'Morning Fletch.' He gave a cursory greeting as he knocked on the Private door. A little green bulb - a new addition to the facilities - glowed over the door - signalling for him to go in.

Christine looked up from her desk as he closed the door behind him. She presented a cheek for him to kiss. 'Morning Chris. The new sign's up. Looks great.'

Christine was unimpressed. 'Yes. But when are you going to get these monstrosities down?' She indicated the Sybil Waite nude murals behind her, with a stab of a gold pencil in their direction.

Soon as I've done the new ones we talked about. That's what I've been working on all morning. They're going to be terrific.'

Christine snapped edgily. 'No! Now. Today. I want them out of my sight.'

Peter withered visibly. 'But the wall behind them is rough. It'll look awful until the new ones go up.'

'Then get it painted! I can't stand this bloody blackness, anyway. I'll have it all done. Red. Yes, I'll have it blood-red. Get it organised. Peter. Today.'

Peter was demoralised. 'If that's what you want. You're the boss.'

'And another thing. When you've taken these girls down, I want them burned.'

'Burned?'

'Yes, burned. And tell me when you've seen them burned and there's nothing left but ash.'

'If that's what you want.'

'Don't keep saying "If that's what you want". I wouldn't say it if it wasn't. Right, I'll take you to lunch.' It was just as if a man were inviting a woman, not the other way round.

Peter moved to open the door for her. 'Wasn't it your sister's wedding this morning?'

'Yes. I sent a present. Fletch rang and told her why I wasn't coming. The publicity could easily have spoilt the occasion for her. It's her day. I didn't want to take the spotlight.'

It sounded like a trumped up excuse to Peter. She could easily have gone without the Press knowing. He was sure that the real reason was that since Sybil's death the twins had seen hardly anything of each other. But he said nothing. That summed him up completely, he thought to himself ruefully.

The girl on the settee recognised Christine at once. Christina Lane looked exactly as she had imagined. Smart, sophisticated, the successful career girl to her long fingernail tips. The girl stood respectfully, smiled sweetly and arched her back to define her breasts more sharply.

'Miss Lane?'

Fletch interjected. 'I explained you're busy. But she -'

'She insisted on waiting. I know the feeling. Come in, dear. Peter, wait a moment, will you? I shan't be all that long.'

Peter looked despairingly at Fletch. It was as near as he'd ever come to protesting.

'Close the door.' The girl obeyed as Christine noted the way she moved, turned; how her legs looked from the back.

'You want to be a model, I suppose?'

'Oh, yes, Miss Lane. Very much.'

Christine went behind the desk and faded up the hard-focus spot on the master panel.

'Don't avoid the light. Let me have a good look at you.'

The girl stepped into the white beam, looking awkward. She was certainly inexperienced, this one. Christine surveyed her quietly for a moment.

'Let me have a look at your figure.'

The girl was hesitant. 'You mean, take my dress off?'

'Not just your dress. Everything.'

Down to bra and pants?'

'Bra and pants, too. We are in the model business. Girls are our stock-in-trade, not undergarments.'

'I've never stripped before.'

'Not even for your boyfriend?'

'Well, they don't strip you completely, do they? I mean, mine doesn't.'

'We needn't go into that! Do you really want to be a model or not?'

'Oh, yes!'

'Well then, see that chair? I want everything you're wearing on that, and you back here, in one minute. I'm a very busy person.'

'Yes, Miss Lane.'

The girl turned like a slave and began to unbutton her dress with trembling fingers. Christine watched her, stroking Sybil's coiled paper-weight without knowing it. Her other hand opened the drawer and took out the same type of form that Sybil completed for her not all that long ago.

'Come along. You'll have to learn to strip quicker than that if you break into this business. Time is money, you know.'

The girl's fingers at last released her bra strap and Christine's eyes widened to see her lovely breasts revealed - as lovely as her own.

As the girl was about to pull down her black briefs, she hesitated. Christine asked: 'You are prepared to do nudes, of course?'

The girl came into the light, her breasts nodding as she walked. Christine pointed to the briefs with the end of the tape measure.

'I said nude. Completely. Now stop being coy and take them off. Or get dressed again and stop wasting my time.'

The girl was near to tears. Her fingers gripped the briefs again.

'It's up to you. You said you wanted to be a model,' Christine repeated. 'But you're not going the right way to prove it.'

Slowly the briefs came down.

Christine approached with the tape measure. 'Just your statistics for the record. Thirty-four.' The tape went round her waist. 'Twenty-three.' she knelt in front of the girl and dropped the tape to her hips. 'Thirty-three.' She rose slowly, taking the girl's hands. 'What's your name?'

'Sybil.'

Christine started. 'Sybil?'

'Yes, Miss Lane. Sybil New.'

Christine didn't hear. She wasn't really listening. Her eyes were fixed on something she could see inside the girl's wrist. A birthmark. The birthmark. Just like Sybil's. Her scream was shrill, piercing. The girl jumped in fear and backed away. Another scream, as for the first time Christine realised what the shape reminded her of. The coiled-snake on the desk.

Christine grabbed the paperweight and hurled it wildly at the girl. It missed her but it nearly hit Peter as he dashed in.

He grabbed at the frantic Christine.

'Sybil! Go away! Leave me alone! Get out!' Christine had gone berserk, screaming and flailing her arms. Her eyes were wide, staring, mad.

The girl clutched her clothes and ran out into Reception, terrified.

But to Christine it seemed as if she was still in the room. It was all Peter and Fletch could do to hold her.

'Keep her away from he! For God's sake Sybil, leave me alone!'

She shook herself free and sprawled face down across her desk, sobbing as if she would never stop. The form she was going to fill in for the new girl was soaked with her tears.

Peter and Fletch exchanged a meaningful look.

Christine's words were hardly comprehensible. 'Sybil - go away, for God's sake, go away!'

Miss Fletcher bent over her. 'There's no one here, dear. No one at all. Are you feeling ill? Shall I call a doctor?'

'Leave me. Just leave me.'

Another look passed between Peter and the secretary. Peter slipped quietly out of the door. Miss Fletcher hesitated a moment longer.

'Oh, by the way - the men have gone. Do you want to go down and have a look at the sign? It's super.'

Christine didn't even raise her head from the desk to shake it. Fletch sighed. I'll be outside if you need anything.'

The door closed and at last, Christine looked up. She stared round the studio with its windowless blackness. It was claustrophobic. All encompassing. Closing in.

She tried to pull herself together. This was what she had strived for, what she wanted, above all else.

But she was alone, Except for her conscience...and Sybil.

Countess Dracula

by Michel Parry

"Reluctantly, they parted their bodies. Her hand found his and held it tightly as he hesitated in the doorway. He blew her one last kiss and was gone.

The *Countess* moved slowly to the small window and peered up at the vivid moon. Her cheeks were flushed red with excitement and apprehension. She bit her lip to stop it quivering.

Tomorrow, she foresaw, she would feast on his young body. And she would make love as she had not done in twenty years."

Filmed by Hammer this story is loosely based on the infamous Countess Elizabeth Bathory, the real life vampire who bathed in the blood of virgins in order to preserve her youth.

Price £7.99   RBKS 001

SPECIAL ILLUSTRATED EDITION

Little Orphan Vampires

by Jean Rollin

"Now they wanted to find a throat to cut, a tender stomach to slit open with their sharp teeth, a plump pair of buttocks for them to sink their fangs into, like hungary young wolves. Just thinking about it made them lick their purple lips with their pink tongues. It was as though they already felt the hot, sticky liquid flowing down inside them...
Their eyes, filled before with the simple joys of seeing, now became cruel and alert like those of night-hunting beasts. The *little orphan vampires* dragged themselves up onto the cemetery wall and looked down over Paris..."

Film director Jean Rollin's latest vampire saga — due for release in 1996, is based on this book which he also wrote. First English edition.

Price £7.99   RBKS 004

SPECIAL ILLUSTRATED EDITION